THE BEARWOOD
WITCH

The ghost didn't look evil. It looked mundane. But Duncan could feel the stinking cold reaching from it – the air around him, touching his skin, so cold that it burned; and he felt a stink reaching down into his throat, so rancid that he retched. He held his breath and couldn't pray, expect in his mind. He stared at the thing fixedly, stared until his eyes hurt, and repeated in his mind: *Our Father, Our Father, Our Father…*

Also by Susan Price in Point:

Point

SUSAN PRICE

THE BEARWOOD WITCH

■ SCHOLASTIC

Scholastic Children's Books
Commonwealth House, 1–19 New Oxford Street,
London, WC1A 1NU, UK
A division of Scholastic Ltd
London ~ New York ~ Toronto ~ Sydney ~ Auckland
Mexico City ~ New Delhi ~ Hong Kong

First published in the UK by Scholastic Ltd, 2001

ISBN 0 439 99511 6

Typeset by TW Typesetting, Midsomer Norton, Somerset
Printed by Cox & Wyman Ltd, Reading, Berks

10 9 8 7 6 5 4 3 2 1

1
NUMBER FIFTEEN

"Where's Saint Etheldreda Street? You know?" The man, interrupted as he was passing, stopped short, and looked puzzled.

"Saint Etheldreda Street," Zoe shouted at him.

His face cleared. "Straight down here, love. First left. Can't miss it."

"Great." Her rucksack slung on one shoulder, Zoe walked away from the bus-stop, leaving behind her the busy junction, with its traffic lights, buses and streaming cars, its big pub and dozens of little, busy shops. The winter's afternoon was already dark; shop windows shone yellow light on to wet, shining pavements and car headlights dazzled.

The narrow pavement outside a big, open-fronted fruit and veg store was choked by crates and sacks of carrots, onions, caulis, and people stopping to gossip and read the prices. Getting past by stepping into the road was impossible because of the steel barriers along the kerb, and it was necessary to push and squeeze and step over pushchairs.

Beyond the greengrocer's was a Victorian school building of dark-red brick with big windows shining and teacher's cars parked in the playground. Beyond that, a video store, a butcher's, a baker's, and a shop called "Magik World" which sold runes, crystals and tarot-card readings.

A smaller street turned off, a zebra-crossing on its corner. High on the brick wall above hung a hoarding which clicked round in sections, changing from an advert for a car, to one for a bra, and then to one for a building society. Beneath it was a sign: St Etheldreda Street.

Zoe looked down a long, straight street of old houses, each house joined to the next, an unbroken line into the distance of grimy brick, doors and windows. And cars. And litter.

Cars and vans were parked down either side of the street in lines almost as unbroken as the houses, leaving only a narrow space down the centre, wide enough for a single car. The litter, as she walked up the street, was under her feet and curling round her ankles: flapping, wet newspapers, old crisp packets, cigarette cartons, fast-food trays and their greasy wrappings, silver foil from chewing-gum and torn, shiny cellophane. The concrete of the pavement was spotted with round, pale spots of chewing-gum trodden flat.

Some of the houses had numbers on the doors. The one she wanted had a decorative scroll of ironwork on the wall beside the door, giving the number: 15.

The bricks had been painted over in a harsh, dark maroon, while above the door an arch of keystones had long ago been painted white, but was now chipped and yellowing. A large glass panel formed most of the front door, but both the glass and the white woodwork were dirtied by rain.

The tiny front yard was separated from the pavement by a low and straggling hedge of privet. Sweet papers and ice-cream wrappers lodged among the leaves and twigs, while empty cans and hamburger trays had wedged among the bushes' trunks at the base.

Zoe pushed open the iron gate and, with one wide step, crossed the cracked grey flagstones of the little yard. The large bay window to her right was obscured by drawn curtains. In front of the curtains, behind the glass, a large grey cat lay curled and sleeping.

The frosted glass panel in the front door was

covered by a pink blind, the pink of fabric sticking-plasters. There was a doorbell, covered by a piece of black plastic tape. Zoe looked for a knocker, but there was only a letterbox at the bottom of the door.

So she knocked on the frosted glass with her knuckles, and waited. The cat behind the bay window raised its head, opened large yellow eyes, and yawned. Zoe looked down the length of the street, watching a bus chugging slowly along the narrow space between the lines of parked cars. On the nearest lamppost hung an overflowing litter-bin and, from its crammed mouth, a brightly coloured packet went flying away on the wind. The same gust of wind, damp and chill, made her shiver.

No one came to the door. She knocked again, hoping that the woman she'd come to see wasn't out. It would have been more sensible to phone first, she supposed, but she'd only been given an address, no phone number.

She knocked again. She wasn't going home without seeing the woman. If she had to, she would sit down here, on the wet, mossy brick wall that divided this yard from the next, and wait until Elizabeth Beckerdyke came home, if it meant waiting all night.

As she raised her hand to knock again, there was a noise from behind the door. The pink blind rattled slightly against the glass, and the door was pulled open.

A tall, broad woman filled the frame of the door. She was dressed in black: a black T-shirt, fading to dark grey, and a long, limp, black woollen skirt, spotted with pilling and lighter bits from washing. She stood very straight, this woman, and held her head up and slightly tilted back, so that she really did look down her nose.

The woman wasn't small or dainty, or young. She was hefty, and it was a broad, full, fleshy face, with dark hollows under the eyes, and deep lines from nose to mouth. All of the features were large. A long, straight nose, all the better to stare down. A wide, full-lipped mouth. Very large, very dark eyes, with large, rounded upper lids. A great mass of crinkly, wiry dark hair drawn back behind her head, not stylishly, but simply tied out of the way. The hair was almost equally divided between black and white streaks.

The woman simply stood there, in the open doorway, staring at Zoe down her nose, until Zoe realized that she was waiting for her to speak.

"You Elizabeth Beckerdyke?"

The woman's eyes opened slightly in surprise, and her brows lifted a little, but she quickly made her expression blank again and continued to look at Zoe. The cat from the windowsill appeared at her feet, and lifted its beautiful lion face, with its round yellow eyes, to Zoe. It was even larger than she'd thought, seeing it on the windowsill, and its grey, tabby fur was longer and fluffier. Mewing, it twined and rubbed itself round its mistress's ankles. The woman said, "I am Mrs Beckerdyke. Who are you?"

"Zoe Hutchinson."

"Are you indeed?"

Zoe said, "Is it right you're a witch?"

The woman's large, brilliant dark eyes blinked once, slowly. The cat at her feet stretched and walked away, passing Zoe on its way to the street. Then Elizabeth Beckerdyke said, "Who told you I was a witch?"

"Lots of folk. They said—"

"Who? For instance?"

"Oh –" Zoe tried to remember the names of people she had no intention of seeing again. "Dorothy Bailey. Her said her knowed you. And this woman – her does readings – lives over by Holly Hall –"

"Oh, those people," Elizabeth Beckerdyke said. "I see. I don't think I have anything to say to you."

Zoe slammed both hands against the door before the woman could close it. Her rucksack slipped from her shoulder and fetched up, with a jolt, in the crook of her elbow. "You've got to see me."

"I don't have to do anything."

"I come special. *Please*."

"Go away."

"I…" Zoe, feeling the tears coming, tried to hold them back, but needed her strength to struggle with the woman and the door. "I…" She collapsed against the door, her weight holding it back, and her whole body jerked as she sobbed, noisily, wetly. "You've got to help me, you're the only one can help me," she said, without thinking about her words. "I shall go mad if you don't help me." She was sobbing and gasping so much that nothing of what she said was comprehensible.

The door was pulled wide open and she staggered, only saving herself by stumbling over the doorstep into the house, catching at the wall beside the door.

"Come in," Elizabeth Beckerdyke said.

The front door of the house opened right into the front room, but Zoe didn't see it, her eyes being full of tears and her hands over her wet face.

"Through there," Elizabeth Beckerdyke said and pushed her through another door into a tiny, square hall, and then through a third door into the back room. Zoe, blinded by tears, moved forward a step and banged her thigh painfully into the wooden arm of a sofa. She gasped and, bent double, tottered a couple of steps more into the clear centre of the room, where, for a while, she gave herself up to weeping: shaking and gulping, gargling, yelping, with tears wetting her face as thoroughly as if a glass of water had been thrown at her. Her rucksack fell from her arm to the floor.

Elizabeth Beckerdyke stood just inside the room, arms folded, watching.

Zoe, aware of time passing and wasting, managed to quieten herself and straightened, wiping at her face with her hands. She was dimly aware of being in a small, dowdy room; of limp curtains, covered with a large pattern of flowers, of a computer in the corner; of worn old chairs crammed together. And there was the woman, Beckerdyke, waiting for her to speak again. Zoe knew that she had to speak to some effect. She had to make her words count. Just when she should have felt strong and together, she felt weak and scattered, and needed help. Reaching into her pocket, she took out a packet of cigarettes and opened it.

"You won't smoke in my house, thank you," said Mrs Beckerdyke.

Zoe frowned, her first impulse to answer angrily. People were always picking on her. And moaning on and on about a bit of cigarette smoke until it made her sick. But she couldn't afford to offend this woman. "I need a fag, I'm upset. Only one."

"There's the door," said Elizabeth Beckerdyke, gesturing towards it with one large arm. "You can smoke as many as you like outside in the street. But you're not stinking my house out."

Zoe closed the cigarette packet, but shook it in frustration, so the cigarettes rattled and rustled inside. "I *need* a fag. Look, you've got to help me."

Beckerdyke shook her head. "No. But you can relieve my curiosity by telling me what this is about."

"My boyfriend. He was in this car. This car."

"Ah." Mrs Beckerdyke, her arms still folded, nodded. "And he was killed. So you've been running to Dorothy Bailey and all those others, asking them to contact him on the other side."

Zoe, her face squeezing into a rubbery clown's grin, nodded. Fresh tears ran down her nose.

"And they told you – oh!" Beckerdyke put her hands to her head, and looked as if she'd been slapped. "There's a spirit coming through. Oh, it's a young man, a young man with dark hair –"

Zoe, her face eager, nodded again.

"Says his name is – can't quite catch it – I think it's – it's – John, is it?"

"Gary," Zoe said.

"Oh, that's right, that's what the spirit's saying, *Gary*. He's quite tall. And good-looking."

Zoe nodded hard. The woman could speak to the dead. And she'd been told that this woman was the best – the *best*. All Zoe's hopes soared. She could forgive the woman any amount of snottiness if she could, if she would, do as Zoe asked.

"It's a trick," Mrs Beckerdyke said, "called cold

9

reading, and every fraud like Dorothy Bailey does it. I guessed that your young man was dark-haired, and I was lucky. He had to be either dark-haired or light-haired. A fifty-fifty chance. And I'm on a pretty good bet in guessing he was tall, and even if he looked like a toad, you'd agree that he was good-looking, especially now he's dead." She observed Zoe's face as it squeezed out of shape again and more tears came. "As for the name, always pretend the spirits are muttering and you can't quite hear. Guess at a few common names, and if you don't guess it right, the subject will like as not tell you – as you did. If they haven't already told you, and forgotten that they did."

"They told me lots of things!" Zoe's arms were waving again. "Things they couldn't know. Couldn't have guessed. It's real! It really is!"

Elizabeth Beckerdyke sat beside a small table on a straight-backed chair. "Of course," she said, and put her hands back to her temples. "Let me see. Let me tune in to the spirits properly. You were engaged, you and – Gary. You were thinking of getting married next year."

Zoe studied the woman suspiciously, while she unthinkingly opened the cigarette packet again, and took out a cigarette. Elizabeth Beckerdyke lowered her hands and stared up into Zoe's face with her large, dark eyes, in which brilliant points of light gleamed.

"You wanted to set up house together, but Gary didn't have a job, so it was difficult."

Hope rose in Zoe again … but the smirk on the woman's face was unsettling. "How do you know that – if –?"

"I'm guessing!" Beckerdyke said, grimacing and shaking her head in exasperation. "It isn't hard, for God's sake. You were obviously attached to the boy and you have a cheap ring on your finger. Most young couples want to set up home together. Many young men these days are unemployed. If I'd been wrong about anything, I would just have said that I'd misheard the spirits and guessed again until I did get it right. And you want to believe so badly – I can see it in your face. That's what makes cold reading easy – no matter how badly you guess, people want to believe you so much. They'll make all sorts of excuses for you, and believe any excuse you give them. I once sat and listened to Dorothy Bailey take eleven tries to guess a sitter's zodiac sign. The sitter still went away believing in her." She looked at her visitor's blank, wet face and wondered if the girl even knew what a zodiac sign was, let alone understood the point she was making. Why, she wondered, do I bother to talk to people? "Don't light that cigarette. I've told you, I won't have smoking in my house."

Zoe looked down at the cigarette and lighter in

her hands. She was quite unaware of having taken them out. Impatiently, she shoved lighter and cigarette back into her pocket without bothering to return the cigarette to its packet.

"They sent you to me as a joke, girl," Beckerdyke said. "A joke on you and a joke on me. Because I've seen their performances, and seen through them, and exposed them. As frauds."

"You're no use to me then," Zoe said. "You're not a witch?"

Elizabeth Beckerdyke's face lost its expression of amusement. "I'm no use to you, no. I *am* a witch. *They* are frauds."

"Then you've got to help me," Zoe said. She still stood in the centre of the room, her arms held stiffly down by her sides. Her right hand, in her pocket, gripped the lighter and loose cigarette. "You've got to."

"To do what? Talk to your boyfriend? Have him say he still loves you, and he's watching over you? Better go back to Dorothy Bailey, my girl. She makes it up as she goes along but she knows all the right things to say."

"That's not—"

"If I worked for you, it would be the real thing. I might not find your boyfriend at all – the dead outnumber the living, and I give no guarantees. That's why people prefer the frauds."

"Yes, but what I want—"

12

Elizabeth Beckerdyke, raising her voice only slightly, easily talked the girl down. "If I did get through to your boyfriend, it would be him speaking – from the other side of death. Not Dorothy Bailey mouthing all the saccharine inanities you want to hear. You might find what he has to say unpleasant. Disturbing. It might not be what you want to hear."

"You're not listening," Zoe said. So many people didn't listen. Gary always had. "I don't just want to speak with him. That's why they sent me to you. I want more than to speak with him."

Elizabeth Beckerdyke looked at her.

"I want him back."

2
SAINT ETHELDREDA STREET

"Sit down," Elizabeth Beckerdyke said.

Zoe looked behind her and saw a large, grey sofa; the sofa she'd banged her leg on when she'd first come into the room. She sat on the edge of it and looked at the witch.

"Let me understand this," said Beckerdyke. "Your boyfriend is dead."

"That's right."

"He was killed in a car crash."

Zoe nodded, her face creasing up again. "They was still cutting him out of the wreckage."

"But you want him back again?"

"I want him back! I don't want just to talk to him, and him saying that he loves me and watches over

x

14

me, and all that. I've heard all that and it doesn't help. I want him –" She slapped the cushion beside her on the sofa. "I want him here. I want his arms round me. I miss him. When I get up in the night and it's cold, and I get back to bed, I want him to be there to cuddle me and warm me up. I want him to be there. I want him. I want him."

"It would be easier," Beckerdyke said, "to get another boyfriend."

"But I don't! I don't! I want – !" Zoe shook her head, unable to speak, and sobbed again, bending over her knees, shaking and gasping for breath.

Beckerdyke watched her for a few moments, then rose and crossed to a single armchair that stood opposite the sofa, in front of the computer. She sat down and leaned back comfortably. With one foot she pulled towards herself a small, white, formica table, which ran across the carpet on wheels, until it was close enough for her to prop both feet on it, ankles crossed. She had large feet, in battered moccasins.

When Zoe could speak, she said, "Everybody keeps telling me to get somebody else. But I couldn't find nobody better than him. Not for me. And when I think. That. I'll never. Ever. See him again. I can't bear it! I can't."

"Few people can," Beckerdyke said. "You have not the smallest idea, not the least perception, of what you're asking, do you?"

"I just want him back."

"What do you want back? A rotting corpse, to put its arms round you? An embalmed one, soaking the bedsheets with embalming fluid?"

"Don't!"

"A ghost won't be able to hug you."

"There must be a way. There's got to be a way. They told me you could do it. They said you were really powerful. The best. That you'd studied. That you knowed things nobody else knows. Please."

Pleasure struck Beckerdyke through before she was prepared for it. She sat quietly, enjoying these words. Dorothy Bailey, and all that crowd, hated her, and were jealous of her, and feared her – and yet still they had to admit that she was their superior. They lit their candles, making a great fuss about lighting the right coloured candle on the right day, as if it made any difference. They bothered about their bits of crystal, and went on about their "energies" and "vibrations", when their bits of rock were mostly quartz or silicon, whatever colour they happened to be, or whatever name they were called by. They spread their bits of printed pasteboard and made up their herbal concoctions – and all the time they missed the bigger picture altogether. They were messing about in a rock-pool and not even noticing the ocean – which was not only foolish, it was dangerous.

"Why don't you sit down," she said, pointing to the sofa, "and tell me about your Gary?"

Zoe looked at the sofa and felt helpless – tired and unhappy and in need of a cigarette. She couldn't pull her thoughts together. "I need a fag. I really need a fag, honest."

She'd hoped that Beckerdyke would relent and let her smoke one in the house, but the woman only gestured to a door behind her. "The kitchen's through there. To your right's the door into the back yard. You can smoke out there."

"Thanks," Zoe said, not sounding thankful at all. She kicked the rucksack which lay on the floor at her feet. "Can I leave this here?" Beckerdyke nodded and Zoe, stepping over the rucksack, went out into the kitchen.

It was a narrow, dingy place. A large dresser on one side, cluttered with jars and packets, and the gas-stove on the other, took up almost all the room. A black plastic rubbish bag, full and spilling over, leaned against the cooker's side. A stainless steel sink in the corner was filled with dirty crocks. The floor under her feet, as she tried to reach the door into the yard, clattered with dishes holding cat-food, milk, water, biscuits. The door, as she opened it, collided with the dishes, spilling what they held.

The door opened into a narrow space, surrounded by walls and paved with broken blue brick, through which grass, weeds and moss grew. It was overlooked by the window of the room she'd just left, but the curtains were drawn.

Turning her back to the window, Zoe took the loose cigarette from her coat pocket, put it in her mouth, and lit it. She took a deep drag, already feeling relief.

She was looking down a long, narrow garden. The kitchen, and a further continuation of the house straggled about halfway along it. The blue brick path continued, until it was overwhelmed by grass and disappeared among tussocks. From about the middle of its length the garden was a complete disorder of long grass, old rose-bushes, other over-grown bushes, weeds and hedges growing over the gardens on either side. At the bottom of the garden could be seen the tower of the Roman Catholic church and the back walls of the shops that fronted the main street where she'd got off the bus. She could hear the traffic, buzzing and droning.

She smoked until her cigarette was down to a stub, then dropped it on the blue bricks of the yard, scrubbing it into the grass and moss with her foot, before letting herself back into the kitchen. Stepping over the cat's dishes, she went back into the sitting-room. Elizabeth Beckerdyke was still sitting in her armchair, her feet up on the little coffee-table, looking through a magazine of television listings. When Zoe entered, she looked up.

Zoe crossed the room, stepping over her ruck-sack which still lay in the middle of the carpet, and sat down on the sofa. "Gary," she began. "I don't know what to tell you. He was only nineteen." She rested her face in her hand, pressing her fingers against her eyes.

"A good boy, was he?" Beckerdyke asked.

"He was lovely. Kind to everybody. He'd give anybody anything, do anything for anybody. He was so good to his little brothers and sisters. Always buying 'em things and giving 'em pocket money. And he was – he was –" Zoe's eyes squeezed shut again, her mouth grimaced.

"So generous," Beckerdyke said. "And yet he was unemployed."

Zoe's eyes opened. "He was generous with what he had. And he made a bit of money from time to time."

"I'm sure he did," Beckerdyke said. "A little burglary here. A car radio ripped out there. Some lead from a roof."

Zoe took her hand from her face, sat up straight and looked across the room at the woman. "Is this another trick?"

"It's true, isn't it? Isn't it true that the car he was killed in was stolen?"

"How do you know?" Zoe's expression flickered between fright and anger. And hope.

"I looked in your bag."

"You looked in my bag!" Reaching out, Zoe snatched up the rucksack and opened it.

"You left it there. Lovely photographs. How I admire the tattoos on his arms. Did he do them himself?"

Zoe, her face baffled, tried to puzzle out how the woman's serious tone should be taken.

"Since you assure me that he was good-looking, I can only suppose he wasn't photogenic."

Zoe, not understanding the word, squinted with suspicion.

"I'm quite touched that you kept clippings of all his court appearances. How proud of him you must be."

"You bitch!" Zoe said.

Beckerdyke smiled. "I imagine the clipping about the joyriders killing themselves and injuring the other driver was about the crash he was killed in? I can't think why you'd have it folded up with all the others and kept inside the funeral card if it wasn't. Were he and his friends drunk when they went joyriding?"

"All right! I never said he was a bloody saint, did I? He nicked a few things. But he was *good*. He never hurt anybody!"

Beckerdyke gave a small laugh. "Except the driver of the other car. Did he survive, do you know?"

"That was an accident!"

"Oh, certainly it was. Our Gary chose to get drunk. Then he chose to steal a car and drive it, drunk. And crashed it. And hurt another driver. Pure accident."

"He wasn't driving!"

"Of course, that makes all the difference in the world."

Zoe, uncertain of exactly what the woman meant, glowered across the room at her. "If you keep on, I'll put one on you."

Elizabeth Beckerdyke didn't move from her relaxed position. "If you so much as raise a hand to me, my girl, you'll wish you'd never been born."

Zoe collapsed across her own knees, sobbing. "He was good. He was *good*. I've got to have him back. Why won't you *help* me?"

"Now it's well-rid of him, I hardly think the world needs the return of a petty thief. And manslaughterer."

"You bitch you bitch you bitch you!"

"That's right," Beckerdyke said, with another laugh. "Sweet-talk me."

"I haven't got any money!" Zoe shouted, her face red and wet. "I spent all the money I had, didn't I, on a headstone. With his picture on it. But I bet you'd do it if I had the money."

"No, dear. I daresay you can be bought for much less than the price of a headstone, but nobody can buy me."

"Who would want to?"

"Oh, that sweet talk."

"Truth is," Zoe said, standing up, "you *can't* do it. No more than them others can. You don't know nothing more than they do. You can't do it. I dunno why I was ever fool enough to think you could." She looked round at the dim little room, with its cheap, ugly curtains and its polystyrene ceiling tiles, and the wallpaper hanging in strips where the cat had clawed it. "If you was a real witch, why would you live in a *dump* like this? Why would you wear clothes like *them*?"

Beckerdyke laughed. "Because, my dear, 'gross gold from me runs headlong to the boor'."

"Eh?"

" 'So is every scholar poor.' "

"You're barmy," Zoe said. "You sit there – in this *dump* – in your ratty old clothes – and *talk* about what you can do and how clever you are, but you can't do nothing. You're useless. You're no good. And I hope you drop dead."

Beckerdyke smiled, but felt a pique she had not expected to feel. Such playground jibes shouldn't nettle her, but it was nevertheless intolerable to have this ignorant little guttersnipe waltzing away down the road, thinking that Elizabeth Beckerdyke couldn't make good her boasts. Probably she would run back to Dorothy Bailey, with all her comforting lies, and tell her that Elizabeth

Beckerdyke was a barmy woman who lived in a dump and "couldn't do nothing". And wouldn't Dorothy Bailey be triumphant? As Zoe turned to the door, her bag in her hand, Beckerdyke said, "You had better be sure, very sure, that you want your Gary back before you ask me to raise him."

Zoe turned back again. "I've been telling you. I am sure. That's all I want. All."

"Well then," Beckerdyke said.

Zoe went back to the sofa and dropped down on it. "I've got no money, and I don't earn much – hardly anything – I just work in this little super-market on our estate, that's all. But I can sell some stuff. I can get some money. I'll do anything."

"Have I mentioned money?" Beckerdyke asked. "This isn't something you do for money."

Zoé looked at her blankly. Everything was done for money.

"Reading palms and teacups. Energizing crystals. Love charms and curses. That's the sort of thing that – *some* people – do for money. This –" Beckerdyke shook her head. "This will be … a demonstration … of power. A proof. A witnessing."

Zoe didn't know what the woman was talking about. "You'll do it? You'll bring him back."

"I want you to be sure," Beckerdyke said. "I want you go away and think, very deeply, very hard, about what you're asking."

"I've thought."

"You haven't. You've dreamed. You've fanta-sized. You've looked for an escape from grief. Do you understand what I'm saying?" The girl's infuriatingly blank, young face showed no sign of it. "I want you to consider what Gary will be. Some consider that every ghost is a demon disguised. If what comes back is merely Gary's shape, Gary's simulacrum, do you still want it? Do you not care what you get, so long as it fills Gary's place?"

Zoe sat clutching at her rucksack, her face screwed up as she tried to consider these things. Demons? Simulacrum? She shook her head.

"And even if what returns is Gary – do you think death won't have changed him?"

"I just. Want him back."

"Go away now," Beckerdyke said. "Don't come back until a week has passed. A week at least. Take longer if you need it. I shall need a week to prepare in any case. Think hard." Beckerdyke kicked away the little table and got up. "Off you go now."

Beckerdyke followed Zoe through into the front room – which she now saw was almost empty, except for an armchair and piles of clothes – and opened the front door for her.

When Zoe turned to say goodbye, she found the door had been closed on her, leaving her in the darkening street.

The lights of the corner-shop glimmered and spread across the wet tarmac. No cars moved: they were all parked along the kerbs. From the end of the street came the quiet clacking of the advert as it turned. A solitary man, carrying a white plastic bag, left the shop and walked briskly away.

Zoe could hear the humming and droning of the traffic from the main road. She could walk round there and lean against the bus-stop outside the tatooist's – and catch the bus and go home.

Where they would ask her, "How are you feeling, love?" And, "Where have you been?" She couldn't bear it.

She could go round to the pub and see if there was any one there that she knew. But why? She didn't want to see them, and they didn't want to see her because they didn't know what to say to her.

There were clubs, but they were too noisy and brash. There was the pictures, but she wouldn't be able to follow the story. Didn't even want to try.

Since she couldn't stand outside the witch's house all night, she stepped through the gate on to the pavement strewn with wet litter, and walked down the long street, passing old, battered doors, and bright, newly painted doors; yards full of rubbish sacks and yards full of flower-tubs and, on the other side, car after car after car.

The street joined a much wider and busier road,

where stood the Abbey, a large pub with brilliantly lit windows and a wide forecourt. Zoe crossed the road to it, and lingered outside, wondering whether to go in, until a man, walking towards the pub's door, grinned at her and said, "Hello, love. Fancy a drink?" Zoe turned away.

The traffic lights at a big junction nearby blinked their jewel colours in the wet night. She turned up a steep hill, passing a big store selling cut-price drink. She had no idea where she was going.

Climbing the long, steep hill left her a little tired, and brought her to a road bordered with tall trees. The pavement had a verge of muddy grass almost covered in wet leaves, all glistening bronze and gold in the light of the streetlamps. She turned aside and scuffed through these leaves, into the longer wet grass. Within a few steps, she felt the chill of water seeping into her shoes. Now she was under the trees. Their trunks, cool grey and green where the light from the lamps reached them, were all round her, and broken twigs and branches were underfoot. She passed by a great fallen tree, its roots upraised in a circle still clotted with earth. Beyond the fallen tree, a wide area of grass suddenly opened, edged with more trees on its further side. The clearing was cool in the dusk and, despite its size, somehow secretive and hidden among the trees.

Zoe hitched herself up on to the fallen tree-trunk and sat there. The trunk was wet, and covered with green lichen and moss which would come off on her clothes, but she didn't care. She wanted to sit down somewhere, and the trunk was better than sitting on the ground in the mud.

The roads and houses that edged this bit of woodland were hidden from sight by the trees, and the noise of the passing cars and buses reached her only as a dim, distant hum. She sat on the tree, looking down the grassy slope as darkness crept out from under the trees, and then she put her head in her hands and cried. She cried because she was filled with hope, and dread, and misery, and was afraid of them all.

She cried quietly at first, but stopped caring how she sounded or who heard her, and her wails and sobs drifted off into the dusk under the trees. Someone passing by, hearing her, might come and ask what the matter was, and if they could help her. She hoped so.

A man went by with his dog, walking briskly, looking straight ahead, pretending not to hear. Zoe cried harder, from loneliness. She'd known that no one would help. No one ever did, not in real life.

3

DUNCAN

The hostel had once been an industrialist's mansion, and the room Duncan shared in it was big, with a large, graceful window, and a high ceiling patterned with plaster wreaths of leaves and flowers. The furniture – three beds, three chairs and three little bedside tables – didn't begin to fill it, leaving wide, cold spaces. The electric light was too dim, making the room full of shadows. Still, it was a step up from the street, and there would be other steps up. There definitely would.

Time was getting on. If he didn't head out soon, he'd be late. His left-over copies of *The Big Issue* he shoved under his bed. They'd be safe enough there. The other guys who shared his room were OK. They left each other's stuff alone.

He put his hand into his jacket pocket, to check that he still had his Bible. It was a small one, about the size of his palm, covered in red plastic made to look like leather. Its pages were tissue thin, their edges gilded with reddish gold – not real gold, obviously, but it looked like it. Every page was printed with the tiniest black letters. It was the best, the most valuable thing he owned, his favourite possession, given to him by an elderly couple, the Robinshaws, who were, possibly, the kindest people he'd ever met. Hard to say, though – he'd met a lot of kind people just lately.

He carried the Bible with him everywhere, but it was especially important that he had it this evening. He was going to his first prayer-meeting.

First, he had to walk there, and it was a bit of a step. But he couldn't throw away money on bus-fares when he could walk. He had to have money to buy more *Big Issues*. And he was saving. Every penny that he could. Because there were definitely going to be more steps up in the future.

So he trudged along the long, long road as the late, dark afternoon darkened further. To his left were pubs and nightclubs and then, later, hotel after hotel after hotel. To his right were four lanes of cars, vans, lorries and buses, all growling along, headlights on. Light rain spattered in his face.

He'd already been on his feet all day, in the centre of town, standing there with his pile of *Big Issues*, so he concentrated on putting one foot in front of the other, and didn't think about how far he still had to go, or how he would get back that night. Just keep walking.

He stopped for a rest in Bearwood, a lively little village trapped on the edge of the city's expanding urban sprawl. The church of Saint Mary the Virgin had a low wall around its yard, and he was able to sit on the wall, and watch the people going in and out of the supermarket opposite, dodging traffic as they ran across the road, queuing for buses, or pulling the shutters down over shops as they shut up.

A few metres down the street was the big corner pub, the Bear, a handsome terracotta building, decorated with bears' heads and large windows which lit the pavements. Underneath the windows were placards, illustrated with a cheery cartoon bear, advertising cheap pensioner's luncheons, live music, a beer garden, happy hours. As he'd passed its door it had breathed out a scent of beer. Just a few months before, he'd have turned into that door, bought a beer, and another, and another – and wouldn't have left until he'd been thrown out. But that had been before he'd met Jesus.

He started walking again. There wasn't that

much further to go. Just up the long hill to Warley Park, and then across the park, and across the busy main road beyond that and the prayer-meeting was being held in one of the houses there. "A bite to eat" had been promised – a promise he hoped would be kept. He was starving.

It was dark under the belt of woodland round the edge of the park, and there weren't many people about. But someone was crying. Someone who didn't care who heard.

He stopped and listened. A child, he thought, who's just fallen down. Mother will pick it up in a minute.

But he knew it wasn't a child. You're just making excuses, he accused himself. So that you don't have to do anything. And that wasn't an option open to him any more.

No child cried like that. It was someone who was very unhappy.

If he offered to help, the chances were that he'd be told to mind his own business, and that would be hurtful and embarrassing. Or, maybe, his offer would be taken up – and it would be even worse, because then he'd actually have to help, and he'd miss his prayer-meeting, and spend his money, and be kept up all night... More excuses, and still whoever it was cried in the darkness.

It really came down to one very simple question: *What would Jesus do?*

The answer to that was easy too. Jesus would go and help. So that was what he had to do. Happily. Willingly. No more excuses.

He picked his way through the trees. The last of the daylight shone, pale, from the wood's edge. It lit, dimly, a great fallen tree, its circle of torn-up roots still holding together a mat of soil. The sobbing came from the tree's other side. He rounded it and saw a girl sitting on the big trunk. She had a rucksack slung on her shoulder, her face was bowed into her hands as she sobbed, and her heels hammered at the tree in a flurry of angry kicks.

Duncan's throat was clogged with embarrassment. He cleared it, but she didn't hear him. What to say? He didn't know, but supposed that anything would do. "Um. All right? Are you all right?"

The voice, coming suddenly from the darkness behind her, startled Zoe, making her heart jump. It was a deep voice. Not a local one. For a moment she was simply glad that someone *had* bothered to ask if she was all right – and then she was angry that anybody had had the brass neck to poke their nose in where it wasn't wanted.

" 'Scuse me," Duncan said, more embarrassed than ever at getting no response, but forcing himself on. "Is something wrong? Are you hurt? Anything I can do?"

Zoe lifted her head and glanced round, but her hands were at her face, wiping away tears, and she only caught a glimpse of a dark figure, a man, standing at a little distance. She snapped, "I'm all right."

"You're greeting," Duncan said.

"I'll be all –" She started speaking angrily, dismissively; but the sobs rose up and overcame her. Ducking her head again, she shook and cried.

Duncan was alarmed, fearing that she was in pain, and he moved closer to her. "What's the matter? Do you need a doctor? I'll help if I can."

Zoe raised her head again, grinning through the tears that ran down her face. "Only way you can help is if you can bring the dead back to life."

"Oh." Duncan edged a little closer to her, leaning against the tree-trunk. "Somebody's died?" he asked gently. He felt an eagerness which was entirely wrong, and pricked him with guilt – but, then again, it was right because this was obviously something he had been sent to do. He had been guided here, to be in the right place to hear this girl crying, so that he could tell her what he now knew – that it was all true. That all the stuff about Jesus and Life After Death that he'd always believed was shite, was real, was true.

At his question she burst out crying again, sometimes shaking her head, sometimes nodding. He was pained by her being so upset, and said,

"Oh. Oh. Don't cry." Reaching out, he shyly but determinedly put his hand on her shoulder.

Zoe was surprised by the touch, even a little offended – but it was so gentle, and so un-expectedly comforting, that she cried harder still.

Duncan felt tears in his own eyes. "I'm sorry. I'm really sorry. Don't mind me asking... Who was it died?"

"My ... my ... my boyfriend."

"Oh. I'm really sorry."

"But never mind." Zoe sat up straight, and drew in shuddering breaths as she wiped her face with her hands, feeling grime from the tree-trunk smearing over her skin. She'd had enough of crying. In the darkness under the trees, the stranger's face was a pale blur, but she got an impression of someone tall and lanky, draped in a shapeless jacket. His dark hair merged into the darkness around him. "I'm getting him back," she said.

Duncan was puzzled. "Er... He's just gone off, then? He's not dead."

"He is. Dead." The girl was a dim shape in the dusk, perched on the tree-trunk. She spoke clearly out of the darkness. "Killed in a car crash. Mashed up in a car crash. Raspberry jam." She was cried out, and it gave her a perverse relief to say these things in a hard, steady voice. "Took hours to cut him out the wreckage. He died while they was working away. With their cutters and torches. Cut cut. Chop chop. And he snuffed it." She snapped her fingers.

He was staring at her, but it was too dark to see his expression. She looked round, noticing how darkness had spread across even the grassy open space below the trees, and she wondered, faintly, if she should be sitting there, in the dark, with this stranger. She wondered, but didn't really care.

"I'm sorry," Duncan said again, bemused. If the boyfriend was dead, how could she get him back? Unless… Was she contemplating suicide, to join him, and get him back that way? His forebodings had been right – he really was getting in over his head here. He had no idea what he should do for the best. But then no one had said that Jesus would only ask him to do easy things.

"You foreign?" she said, wrong-footing him again.

"Eh?"

"Only you got a funny accent."

She could just make out his face moving into a grin. "Aye," he said. "Foreign."

"Irish."

He grinned again. "Scots."

"I could tell you was something. Glasgow?"

"Dundee."

"Oh," she said, without much interest. Glasgow was in Scotland, she knew; but she didn't know where Dundee was, and cared less. "I suppose I'd better be going." She slipped from the tree-trunk to the muddy grass.

Duncan felt a touch of panic. Where was she going, and what was she going to do? "Sure you're all right?"

"I'm OK now. I'm fine."

In the dark she saw him move his head as if he was about to speak – but then he turned his face aside and didn't. Again he made to speak, and again, he stopped.

"What?" she said.

"It's just that – I don't understand. Is he buried abroad, your boyfriend? Or a long way off or something?"

Zoe stared at him. She'd never said anything about Gary being buried abroad. "What you talking about?" She started to walk past him, back to the road.

"Well. You said – I'm sorry –" Duncan kept pace with her, slipping in wet leaves and stumbling on tree roots. It was very dark under the trees now. "You said he was dead, but – you were going to get him back?"

"I've been to see somebody who can do it," Zoe said. It was a pleasure to tell someone, a stranger, who wouldn't tell her she was being stupid and should pull herself together and find a new boyfriend. "A real witch. A real powerful witch.

Her's going to fetch him back. I've got to have him back."

The Scotsman stopped short and, surprised, Zoe stopped too. Water dripped from the trees, and she could feel water seeping into her shoes. She could see nothing of him except his dark shape. He said, "You've been to see a witch?"

"A real un," Zoe said. "Not one of these that just pretend. Her's going to bring Gary back."

Bloody hell, Duncan thought. This is *serious*. Gently, to make sure, he said, "From the dead?"

He sounded impressed, Zoe thought. "Her told me to go away and think about it for a week, to make sure it's really what I want. But I know what I want. I shall go back next week, and her'll fetch him back for me."

"You mustn't do that," Duncan said. No wonder Jesus had steered him here – how wonderful that Jesus had chosen him. "You mustn't, mustn't do it."

Might have known it, Zoe thought. People always poke their noses in, interfering, telling you what to do, even when they're strangers and it's no business of theirs. Walking on ahead down the muddy path, she said, "I shall do what I like." She was pulled up short as the Scotsman grabbed her by the wrist.

"No. Listen. You've got to listen."

Zoe pulled away from him hard, trying to yank her hand out of his. "Gerroff!"

"No, it's all right. I'm not going to hurt you, but you've got to listen. You mustn't do that."

"Let go!"

He let her go, and she took several hurried steps along the dark path, feeling mud and packed leaves under her feet. A glimpse of the road and the lamp-light through the trees made her feel safer. Turning back towards the Scotsman, but still taking steps away from him, she said, "Get stuffed. Drop dead, you nutter."

Duncan raised his hands high, palms out, to show he meant no harm. "OK, I'm sorry, I'm sorry." He was desperate to keep her talking, to get her to listen. "Please. I'm thinking of you. Don't go back to this woman – it's dangerous. Please."

Zoe felt an instant jolt of anger and, in the dark, scowled. "Who says?"

"Jesus says."

"Who?"

"Jesus."

"Ah, piss off!" Zoe said. "Nutter! Go to hell!" She ran for the road. Behind her, she could hear the Scotsman trampling through the soggy leaves and mud, brushing aside twigs and stems. Her shoes clacked on the hard pavement, and then her arm was seized again, and she was pulled up short and swung round, her head snatching back. The Scotsman was there, holding her, shouting.

They were both caught in the pool of flat, white light from a streetlamp, and she saw a thin, pale face, quite young, and dark hair, growing shaggy and wavy. A big, baggy parka enveloped him from shoulders to knees.

"You've got to keep away from people like that!" he shouted. "They're no good. You mustn't –"

Zoe was furious – furious that he was holding her arm, furious that he had the gall to give her orders. She jumped at him, punching with her free fist, kicking, bringing up her knees, all the time swearing. He buckled, backing away from her and bending double.

"You bastard!" she said, punching down at his bent head. "You sod you pig you bastard you!" She took another kick at him, and he fell over on to the pavement and curled up into a ball.

She thought she'd better get away while he was on the ground and, turning, ran as hard as she could down the street, her shoes clacking on the pavement.

Duncan, curled up and smarting on the hard wet pavement, heard her go. He groaned and rolled over, his flesh pinched between his bones and the hard concrete as he sat up. The girl's knuckles, and pointy knee-cap, had caught him on the face and leg, and he rubbed the places, trying to ease the pain, while laughing and shaking his head. She had hurt him, no doubt about it, but he'd been beaten up by experts before now, and he thought he'd survive.

Picking himself up from the pavement, he said aloud, to the parked cars, the streetlamps and the trees, "That's what you get for trying to help people. Ah, well. On we go."

He walked back under the trees and crossed the park. It was almost empty, except for a couple of dogs running loose. The golf course, when he reached it, had been abandoned by the golfers. A long, long line of gleaming headlights bordered the course, marking the main road.

He dodged through the traffic, pausing on the central reservation before running across the further carriageway and entering a cul-de-sac leading off the main road. The buildings there were maisonettes, each set in a small garden, with brick paved paths glistening in the rain. Duncan turned in at number four, and climbed the wet, grey steps leading to the upper floor. The front door was painted a bright violet, and stuck to one of its small glass panes was a fish-shaped sign.

The door was rattled open a few seconds after Duncan's knock by a small, rounded woman in a denim shirt and jeans. She had dark, wavy hair in a short bob, and large, very bright dark eyes. "Duncan! Come on in! You want a cup of coffee? Or would you rather have tea?"

Petra was a fanciable little woman. Married, of course. And a doctor too. No chance of her ever being interested in him. "Er, coffee's fine, thanks." The tiny kitchen – there was just room for him to stand by the door when Petra retreated to the sink – was painted a brilliant egg-yolk yellow, with bright, light-green cupboards and shelves.

"Go through," she said. "I'll bring the coffee. You're a bit early."

"Sorry," Duncan said.

"No, no. It's just that'll you'll be stuck with me for company before anyone else turns up."

"I wasn't sure how long it would take me to get here."

"Oh, you're all right," Petra said. "It gives us a chance to have a natter."

"Am I in the way? Is there anything I can give you a hand with?"

"Oh, *no*!" She waved one hand to dismiss the idea. "Marc's bringing some wine when he comes off shift, and we'll send out for takeaways. There's nothing to do. Like a biscuit?" She held up a packet of chocolate digestives, and Duncan grinned and nodded. He had a sweet tooth and was unable to refuse. "Go through," she said again.

A short, narrow hallway, painted the same brilliant yellow as the kitchen, led to the back of the flat, and gave access to the other rooms. Duncan went through the first door, and blinked at a small room with walls painted bright orange, and the ceiling, door and window frames a light but intense blue. A large framed picture of a sunflower hung on one wall, and, on another, a big silver crucifix. A blue and white chequered throw covered the small, chunky sofa, and a grey armchair had blue cushions. In one corner slumped a dark-blue beanbag.

"Have a seat." Petra came in behind him. "While you can. Most people will be sitting on the floor tonight. Oh, just stick it down anywhere," she said, seeing him looking for somewhere to put his mug down. He sat in the armchair and set his mug on the floor beside his feet. Petra dropped down on the sofa. "Most of the people you'll know," she said, "and you'll soon get to know the others. It's all very friendly, you'll see. Don't worry."

He smiled, acknowledging that he had been worried. "I brought my Bible," he said.

She gave another big smile. "Oh great! Tell you what – have you got a favourite passage? One you'd like to share with everybody tonight?"

"Share?" he said, puzzled.

"I mean, read aloud."

"No!" he said, immediately, emphatically. His face turned hot at the thought of everyone staring at him while he tried to stammer through long, Biblical words and names.

"Oh, that's fine, that's fine, you don't have to, it was just a thought. Hey, have a biscuit. Have two or three."

She leaned over to offer him the packet. He took three, and then a little silence fell. As he dipped a biscuit in his tea, and still nothing was said, Duncan worried that he'd been rude.

"So," Petra said. "What part of Scotland do you come from?"

Normally Duncan would have groaned inwardly at this question, and braced himself for the jokes about kilts, braw bricht moonlicht nichts, and deep-fried Mars bars; but today he was reminded of the other girl who had asked him where he was from, less than an hour before. "Oh. Er. Dundee."

"I don't know Dundee at all," Petra said. "We were in Glasgow a year or two ago. Wonderful place. Wonderful art gallery."

"Yeah," Duncan agreed. He was sick of hearing about how wonderful Glasgow was. "There's nothing much in Dundee."

"Is that why you left?"

Duncan fell silent again, watching the tea rise over the biscuit as he dipped it, making the slightly crinkled chocolate glisten. "More or less." Then he asked himself why he was being so cagey. These were the best people he'd ever found, weren't they? They were part of his new life with

43

Christ, weren't they? And of course they wanted to know about him, since they were taking him into their community. "My mother died –"

"Oh, I'm so sorry."

That's what he'd been saying to that girl. "I'm so sorry, I'm really sorry." Aloud, he said, "It was a long time ago. I was only about eight. I lived with my dad. My step-dad, really."

Petra stiffened in her seat, and her face became more attentive. The reactions were tiny, barely noticeable, but he picked up on them because he'd seen them before. She was expecting some story about how his step-father had viciously beaten him every day. "He was all right, my dad. I'd always got on with him. But after my mam died, he just... He got a wee bitty – down."

"Oh, poor man."

"It was funny, he was all right at first. Seemed to cope. But then, instead of getting better, he got worse. Went downhill. Drank more and more. Started gambling. There was never any money. He'd be sitting about the house, staring at nothing, or greeting."

Petra shook her head, frowning, and made a tutting noise.

"I was doing everything. Looking after meself. Shopping, cooking, washing. I was doing part-time jobs – delivering newspapers, helping with milk-rounds, anything – so I'd got some money of me own. For food. I was trying to sort him out, trying to get the money off him to pay bills –"

"How old were you?" Petra asked.

"Eleven, twelve?"

"I'm surprised you weren't taken into care!"

"I didn't want to be taken into care! No thanks. It wasn't so bad." Duncan looked down at his hands clasped about his mug of coffee. He felt he should leave it at that, and not say anything more. There was no point in complaining about things that were over and done with. But Petra was waiting for him to go on, and once he started, it was hard to stop. "It got on top of me a wee bit. I had teachers at school saying, 'You can do better than this, why don't you buck yourself up?' And I'd go home, and he'd be talking about killing himself… I come home once, and they'd cut the electricity off. He'd said he'd pay the bill with his winnings – he'd sworn he would – and he hadn't. And there was always other bills to be paid… I was phoning up, and going to the offices, saying, 'Don't cut us off,' but they'd say, 'You've got to get your mam or dad to come in, son…' I thought, I'm sick of this. I couldn't do worse than this on me own. I was fourteen. I thought I was big enough. I packed some clothes in a bag, I turned the house upside down and found all the money I could – about eighty quid. And then I just went."

Petra was absorbed in his story, her head

45

propped on her hand. "You had the nerve to do that at fourteen? I was still taking a teddy bear to bed. Where did you go?"

"Here. Birmingham."

"Why? Did you know somebody here?"

Duncan shook his head. "I wanted to come to England. I had this idea that it'd be easier to find a job down here." He pulled a face. "And I wanted to get across the border. It was like, all my problems were in Scotland, and I was going to leave 'em behind."

"But why Birmingham? I'd have thought you'd have gone to London."

"Didn't like the sound of it. No, I got on the first train that was leaving, a big inter-city train. And when I was fed-up being on the train, I got off at the next stop."

"Which happened to be Birmingham?"

Duncan nodded.

"And what did you do? I can't imagine being fourteen and all on my own in a strange city, with nowhere to go."

"I slept rough. I'd done it before. There's been times I'd been a wee bitty pissed off with my dad, and I'd stay away a few days, dossing with friends, or sleeping rough. So I wasn't new to it. And I'd been fending for myself for years."

Petra was leaning forward over her knees, her chin in her hand. "And how old are you now?"

Duncan had to think about it. He hadn't kept a strict count of his birthdays. "Eighteen."

"And you've been living rough all this time?"

Duncan, thinking back over the past four years, nodded slowly. "Been in and out of hostels and shelters. Did this and that to earn money, but it was never enough to save anything. Thought I was going to get a council flat one time, but it fizzled out. See, there's people need housing more than me."

"That's dreadful."

Duncan kept quiet. The account he'd given her had been thoroughly censored, saying nothing of the amount he'd been drinking. It was odd, how he'd prided himself on not being fool enough to get into drugs, on never touching "that stuff", while getting smashed out of his brain on booze almost every day. And throwing up, and falling down, getting into fights, being arrested and thrown out of hostels for pissing the bed, and not having a hope in hell of getting or keeping a job – anyway, wouldn't a job have wasted drinking time? "It's not so bad," he said. "Better than home, in a way. I've only had meself to think about, and only meself to look after. That was easier."

"Didn't your step-father report you missing or try and find you?"

"I don't know. I left him a letter, saying not to worry, I was just heading off. And I've wrote him letters since. Just notes, saying I'm all right. I don't know how he is. Could have drunk himself to death for all I know." He thought of the way his own life was being warmed and lit by the presence of Christ. "I suppose I should try and find out."

"You'd probably feel better if you did," Petra said. "How did you come to the church?"

"It was somewhere to get a cup of coffee and a doughnut on a Sunday morning." She laughed. "No, that's what it was." The hostel he'd been staying in at the time wanted its guests out of their rooms during the day, and walking the streets had been boring, and often cold and wet. He'd seen the notices announcing that a church service was being held in the school hall he was passing, and had wandered in, hoping to sit down for a while, if nothing else. He had been able to sit down for nearly two hours, had eaten two jammy doughnuts and drunk two cups of coffee, and had been entertained by a small band playing songs that were catchy, if not exactly cutting edge. "Everybody was friendly. I started heading over there every week."

The people had been more than friendly. The pastor had started talking to him, because he was new, and, on hearing that he was homeless, had put a hand on his arm and gently steered him aside from everyone. He'd led Duncan over to the table where the money from the collection baskets was being counted, and had quickly sorted out twenty pounds in one and two pound coins. He'd handed it to Duncan, saying, "I think you need this more, this week, than the church does." And, before he'd left, a tall, elderly couple, both with greying hair, had asked him if he'd like to come home to dinner with them. "I always put an extra chicken in on Sundays, just in case we invite someone back," the wife said.

"It'll only be wasted if you don't come," the husband had said. "Come and help us eat it." That was the Robinshaws.

Duncan had refused that week – he'd pleaded an earlier engagement, but, in reality, had been worried that he wouldn't get enough drinking time. But the next week, the invitation was renewed – and wine had been mentioned. Free drink had been irresistible.

Over succeeding months, the Robinshaws had fed him, let him take baths at their house, given him his Bible, and a thick, warm waxed jacket. "I was going to give it to Oxfam anyway," Brian Robinshaw said. "It'd save me the trip if you'd take it off my hands."

Petra tossed the packet of biscuits to him. "Did you go to church before, I mean when you were in Scotland? We always went, ever since I can remember."

"Never," Duncan said. "There was this woman, lived in our street, very religious. Everybody laughed at her. Thought she was cracked." He sat looking into his mug, which was still half-full of coffee. "I thought you were all cracked to start off. And then." He stopped, thinking that he shouldn't say any more. There were some things that, if you tried to put them into words, became more muddled, not clearer.

"And then – what?" Petra said.

"Nothing," he said, but then shifted, fidgety, in the chair. "I had. Well, something happened. It was. Like. An experience."

Petra simply waited for him to go on.

"People kept telling me about God in their lives," he said. "That they knew Christ. I didn't know what they were talking about. Thought they were mad. But they kept telling me that I could find out if I wanted to."

Laura Robinshaw had frequently told him that he only had to ask, and Christ would come to him. He'd told her to her face that she was talking rubbish. She just smiled and said, "But I know it isn't rubbish."

"So one night…" He'd been in a hostel, in a tiny room, with somebody shouting down the corridor, and somebody playing loud music over his head. "…I asked." Embarrassment stopped him from speaking, and he had to swallow. "Well, I asked Christ to come to me." He felt his face grow hot. The words seemed so ludicrous when spoken aloud to someone else. But they were *true*. He could only stand by what was true, and speak it. "I said, 'Come on, then, if you're real. Prove it to me. If you're real, I want you with me. So come on.'"

There was a long silence. Petra, her chin in her hand, didn't move. Eventually she said, "And He came?"

Duncan nodded. But he had to explain. He couldn't leave it sounding as if Christ had knocked on the door and asked if he had a minute to spare. It hadn't been like that at all. And yet Christ had come.

He'd been sitting up on his bed in his tatty little room in the hostel, listening to the noise from down the hall and upstairs, feeling depressed and angry, and he'd been thinking these angry thoughts. *Come on then, if you're real, prove it*. He'd clenched his fists, he'd spoken aloud. "I want You with me, why aren't You with me, why don't You come to me?" The wish behind the words had bitten deep into him, making an ache in his chest.

And then he'd thrown himself on the bed, full length, and looked up at the ceiling. He'd stared so long and hard at the ceiling, with such wide-eyed, dry-eyed anger, that everything had blurred, and he'd still stared furiously into the blurring – and then…

Well, the room had suddenly been crowded.

The air had thickened and grown warm, until the little room was packed with this warmth, this thick, dense air.

He'd felt that a thick, heavy, warm blanket had been thrown over him as he lay on the bed. A wonderfully warm, enfolding, comforting blanket, so heavy that he couldn't move. Couldn't get up, couldn't turn his head. Couldn't lift an arm or a leg. He'd lain there, pinned, a little nervous, but feeling too warm and – well – *held*, to be very frightened. He'd waited to see what would happen next.

What had happened next was that he'd felt light-headed, and then light and floaty... At least part of him had. He remembered what had happened vividly, remembered how it had felt. To describe it in words, even to himself, was so difficult.

Part of him – his body, for want of a better word – had remained weighted down and pinned to the bed. But some other part of him – that light, floaty part – had drifted right up through the heaviness, had risen and floated away from his body, rising towards the ceiling.

He'd felt a brief spurt of fright; but then the sense of warmth and of being held had calmed him, and he'd relaxed. Let it happen. It wasn't going to be anything bad.

So this floaty part of him had floated up to the

ceiling. He'd seen the texture of the paint right up close. And then he'd slowly, easily turned around in the air – like an astronaut turning in a slow-motion float. Over he'd turned, and looked down on himself lying on the bed.

That had been a shock, to see himself lying down there, all spread out, so big and clumsy. But then it had seemed funny. He'd wanted to point at himself and hoot.

"It was like I was looking down on myself," he said to Petra. "And then it was like I could see inside myself."

As he'd looked down on himself, he'd watched his ribcage, and the clothes and flesh covering it become as transparent as glass. He hadn't been surprised. It had seemed natural, like watching a steamed-up window that you couldn't see through slowly become clear.

When it had cleared he saw, inside himself, a red jewel, bright as a traffic-light's "Stop". His heart. There'd been something going on around this red jewel, something unclear, and he'd blinked, and brought his eyes into sharper focus, and then he'd seen.

There were two great hordes, two struggling armies, fighting desperately over and around the red jewel, fighting for possession of it. One army had been of grey and ugly things – fish-mouthed, frog-bodied things – vomiting and shitting as they fought, befouling everything. That was Evil's army – he recognized it as easily as he would recognize a brick. Evil's army, struggling to drag him down into drink and theft and worse, to dirty him and incriminate and destroy him; and to laugh and party and rejoice when they'd won, because his insignificant little heart would be one more point to them.

The other army – he knew them, too. They were Christ's army, fighting with all the strength they had, to save him, because they loved him, and he mattered, and they wanted him – not to score a point, but because his heart was a precious thing to them, even more precious than it was to him.

He couldn't say that to Petra. If he tried, it would just sound stupid.

But, he knew, even if he was suddenly given the words of a poet and the voice of an actor, nothing he could say would come near to describing what he'd seen, and what he'd felt while watching it.

Better to say little or nothing about it, because he couldn't bear not to do the vision justice.

"I could see Christ inside me," he said. "And. I suppose. The Devil." He looked into his coffee mug. He couldn't look at her while saying such things. But he had to say them, because that was what he'd seen. "Fighting for me."

He'd watched the fight with more attention than he'd ever given anything in his life. He'd never before seen anything that was so important. And, as he watched, Christ's army slowly – with great effort, great difficulty – pushed back the grey, ugly army and drove them – slowly, with such desperate effort – out of his heart and away.

Then the little red jewel that was his heart had shone and pulsed and sparkled with such a clean, bright red light as Christ enthroned Himself in it. And then Duncan had felt love; pure love. Such warm, enfolding, secure love wrapping him up tight like swaddling bonds, guarding him, nourishing him. It had pulled him down from his place by the ceiling, like a parent lifting a child safely down from a high wall. He'd been brought down and cuddled back into his body. Lying on the bed again, he'd felt so *safe*. At peace, because he was safe. Relaxed and at ease, because he was safe.

Jesus loves me! The words had seemed twaddle to him before: a silly slogan twittered by people who were in deep shit, and trying to kid themselves that they weren't.

He hadn't understood the words' meaning, that was all. He hadn't understood. Now he understood, the words didn't twitter at all, weren't silly at all. They were a hundred metres high, carved in stone. Their meaning was as simple, clear and strong as granite. Jesus Loved Him.

"Jesus won," he said, and put one hand to his

heart. He didn't care if it sounded stupid, or if the gesture seemed affected. He was stating what he had seen and how things seemed to him as plainly and truthfully as he could. "I know that Jesus loves me." He hadn't had a drink since then, and hadn't needed one. Whenever his thoughts had turned that way, he had thought of the vision he'd seen, and what it meant, and he'd been buoyed up and carried beyond the need for a drink. Drinking seemed silly. Just pointless and silly, something he didn't need to do. Worrying seemed silly. Bothering to be afraid seemed silly. What did any of it matter? Jesus loved him.

Petra was staring at him, her dark eyes even brighter than usual. "Wow," she said. "I've never experienced anything like that."

"Well," he said, and looked down into his mug again.

"You've got to tell everybody about it, tonight. They'll want to hear."

He looked up, aghast. "No!"

"Oh, you must. When something like that's given to you, you've got to share it. I mean, you're privileged. Most of us go through our lives, keeping faith, and never experience anything like that. You can't keep it to yourself."

"No," Duncan said. He stared at the floor, thinking. "When I was coming across the park," he said, "there was a girl. Crying." He remembered her as he'd seen her in the light of the streetlamps, just before she'd hit him. A dark skin – "olive", it was called, wasn't it? Blonde hair, probably dyed, pulled up into a pony-tail on top of her head. A pretty, monkeyish face. "She –" But what the girl had told him was her secret, and not to be told to everybody.

He should help *her*. Not people who were already safely in the church and wrapped in Christ's love. They didn't need his help.

She needed it. She was wandering, lost, outside. She was meeting with a woman who called herself a witch and they were going to mess around, trying to raise the dead.

The woman was mad, most likely, and the girl half-mad. But what they were going to try and do was dangerous.

He'd listened to sermons preached about that sort of thing at the church – about the dangers of using ouija boards, or going to seances. When people tried to call the dead, the dead wouldn't come – but *something* would. Those things he'd seen fighting for his heart – those fish-mouthed, spider-bodied, snake-skinned things – *they* would come, and they'd enter into undefended hearts and live there, like parasites living under your skin.

Once he'd have laughed at the idea, and dismissed those who believed it as cranks, but now he knew. He'd seen it.

"She what?" Petra asked. "What were you going to say?"

"Nothing," Duncan said. But, sitting there, he was awash with shame and guilt. He'd been sent to help that girl. And he'd failed. He'd given up at the first fall.

Christ had fought His way into his heart and, enthroned there, and holding Duncan safe in His arms, He had asked Duncan to help this lost girl and save her from the danger she was in. And Duncan had taken a little stab at it, and then had given up because it got hard.

Sitting there in the comfortable armchair he realized that, instead of staying for the prayer-meeting, and making some new friends, and having a laugh over the takeaways – instead of that, he had to get out into the dark, wet night and find that girl again and help her.

It would be hard. He didn't know the girl's name or where she lived. But there would be a way. Jesus would make sure there was a way.

"You really should tell people about that tonight," Petra said, getting up from her chair. "You'll have to excuse me a minute." She went down the hall to the bathroom.

While she was away, Duncan quietly left by the kitchen door. Once outside, in the dark, with a light, cool rain falling, he ran down the steps, and then ran away down the street before Petra found he'd gone and attempted to call him back. Petra was the first person he'd tried to tell about his experience, and it had been miserable. He wasn't going to tell anyone else. Christ didn't want him to talk. He wanted him to find the girl and help her.

4

ELIZABETH BECKERDYKE

For her journey to the land of the dead, Elizabeth Beckerdyke had first prepared a bag filled with the things she would need on the other side. A sharp knife, a packet of coloured chalks, a bowl, some matches. This bag she kept with her, wherever she was.

For three days she hadn't left her house, not even to go into the back garden. She hadn't switched on the television or radio. When it grew dark she lit candles and drew the curtains. When she had to sleep she blew out the candles – if they hadn't already guttered out – and lay down on the sofa, breathing in the snuffed candles' stink.

In three days, she hadn't eaten anything; nor had she drunk anything except water.

It was hard; but this was what had to be done, to walk with the dead.

Most likely, she thought, the wretched girl won't come back and all this effort will be wasted.

But no, not wasted. A path has to be walked often, to be known, and she had neglected this path. Because it was hard. Even if the girl never came back, it was not wasted effort, this journey.

For the first day, because she wasn't drinking tea or coffee, she'd been plagued by a slight but insistent headache. After that her head cleared; and the sharp emptiness of her belly made her feel alive and strong as she continued to refuse to eat.

Every day she started her work by holding her hands in front of her, fingers spread, concentrating until she could see the buzzing, shining white field of power that surrounded her – a broader and whiter band of light than that which surrounded most people, tinged with violet. By the force of her will, she made it swell broader still, the violet tinge deepening. It would be some protection, like armour, when she left this world.

She sat in her armchair and, for hours at a time, concentrated on everything. The wallpaper on her walls was cream, with a faint embossed pattern which she allowed her eyes to run round, striving to be aware not only of a single block of the pattern, but of the whole pattern as it interlocked to cover the entire wall within her sight. At the same time she was aware of the faint lines where one strip of paper ended and another had been pasted up – and of the little tears, which showed the paper's buff underside, and the creases and the stains.

But, in concentrating on what she could see, other senses fell into abeyance, and that must not be allowed. While retaining awareness of the stains, creases, tears and patterning of the wallpaper, she sought for the sound of traffic from the nearby main road, and found it: a continual, muffled drone.

The drone was made up of many individual vehicles and, concentrating, she heard them: the light, hurried crooning of cars, the heavier chugging of buses; the growling and wheezing of lorries. She heard the heavy bouncing of trucks on manhole covers; the catch and squeal of brakes, a horn sounding – but while she listened for and heard all this, she kept her eyes moving over the wall and never, for a second, lost her awareness of the detail before her – and there was also the gas-fire and, on its top, a hairbrush with hair in its teeth, a bundle of old gas and electricity bills, a corn-dolly, a bottle of whisky and a white, plastic box in which she kept loose change.

The gas-fire added a soft plooping sound to the traffic's noises and the flames burned blue and yellow behind its charred ceramic grille…

Under her hands, the corduroy material that covered the armchair was soft and ridged...

She could feel the soles of her shoes under her toes, and the seams, and through the soles she could feel the hardness of the floor...

From the street outside her front door came the sounds of nearer cars, a car-door slamming, a voice calling out...

From the back yard, the sound of a neighbour's door opening and closing, and the shouting of children in the school playground at the end of the street...

She could smell the dust burning in the fire. Raising her arm to her face, she smelt her own skin, and the scent of her old dress...

She could feel the collar of her dress and her hair against her neck...

While becoming aware of each new thing, she must not lose awareness of all the rest; to be aware, instantaneously, of every single thing there was to be seen, heard, touched, tasted and smelt.

To intensify the concentration like this sharpened it. Her eyes refocused and magnified tinier and tinier details – individual tufts of the carpet's weave, tiny dents in the metal of the gas-fire that caught the light. Her sense of smell refined, and she could distinguish not only the fumes from the gas-fire, and the dusty smell of the armchair, but the soap on her own skin, the soap-powder in her clothes, and the thicker smell of the carpet. Her hearing brought her the twitter of a bird outside, the creak of the stair-door, the wind in the chimney, and the different sound of every vehicle passing on the nearby roads. More light seemed to flood in through her eyes. She felt the small hairs on her arm move in small draughts. She felt her spirit rise in her, its ties to her body loosening...

But the effort of the concentration was too great, too tiring. She covered her eyes with her hands and sighed. Her spirit slumped back into her.

The cat, Simple, was wailing outside the back door. She heaved herself from her chair, trudged through into the kitchen and let him in. At once, he fell on the dishes laid on the tiles, full of cat-food, water and biscuits.

Elizabeth would not eat. She switched on the kettle and, after a moment or two, poured herself a cup of lukewarm water. Returning to her living-room, she put on a tape of drumming. Sitting in her armchair, she sipped water and lost herself in the drum's rapid sound.

On the second day, she plugged the extension lead into the kitchen socket and took the long cable through into the bathroom, where she plugged in the electric fire. When the room had become hot, she ran a hot bath and left it to fill, while she fetched a jug of cold water. Then she soaked in the hot water, in the hot, steamy room, for hours, emptying water out of the bath as it cooled, and re-filling it from the hot tap. She drank cold water when she was thirsty, but ate nothing at all. When she climbed out of the bath, eventually, she was weak, and staggered against the wall while drying herself. She pulled on her dress, and heavy cardigan and tottered through to her living-room, where she sank, exhausted, in her chair.

On the third day her hunger was bad: pressing, nagging. In the cupboard in the kitchen was a large bag of raisins, which she could pull out by handfuls and stuff into her mouth. There were apples and oranges. There was porridge and rice and cans of soup.

But finding the strength of spirit to say, "No!" to the body was the discipline. Weaken the body and the spirit may find the strength to slip free of it.

She was cold, and her movements were slow and feeble, her hands weak and clumsy, as she rose from the sofa and crossed to the gas-fire to turn it on. In the kitchen, it was hard to turn the tap, to pour herself a mug of water – and harder still to ignore the fruit, which she could smell. But she went, slowly, back into the sitting-room, where she put on her tape of drumming, and added whisky to the water in her mug. Sitting in her armchair, sipping at her drink, she once more began to concentrate on everything at once: the pattern and texture and tears and creases of the wallpaper; the sound of drumming; the sound of her own sipping and swallowing, the sensation of swallowing; the traffic-noise; the pressure against her skin of the chair she sat in; the creaking of the house, the heat of the fire…

The light pouring in on her grew brighter. The patterns and textures before her dissolved into a whirl of white light. The sound blurred into it; her spirit rose in her; she flew on the wings of the drumming…

Treading lightly on the air, centimetres above the ground, she moved through the graveyard, passing by the grey stones that leaned to this side and that. Her bag of tools was on her back. She called out, "Cat! Cat! Come!"

The long, wet grass brushed her hovering feet and legs, and she breathed in deeply the scent of mud and leaves and crushed green. A new grave was before her, the earth still bare and soft, and she stood a moment, looking at it. Then, raising her arms, she cried, "Cat! Cat! I come!" She leaped and, like a leaping salmon or dolphin, dived into the earth.

Sticky mud, loose crumbs of earth, filled her eyes with darkness, blinded her. Her mouth gaped, and was filled with earth that forced her jaws further open. She swallowed earth and darkness; the grave entered into her.

The earth flowed over her breast and flanks; her legs kicked in it. Small stones scraped her. Roots caught at her, stroked her. The cold surrounded her and chilled her through. She swam, down into the earth, into the grave.

Down and down, and then rising, then bursting out of the earth, into light. She shook her head and earth fell from her eyes. With her fingers, she clawed it from her ears and mouth, and spat it out, ready to see, and hear, and speak in this new place.

She was in the High Street, just round the corner from her house. She was rising from the concrete and tarmac of the High Street, climbing out of it. There were the streetlamps, and the shops, and the cars and buses going by…

She scratched more earth from her eyes and saw that the tall streetlamps were made of long bones, and the light shining from them was ice-cold and grey.

She reached out to touch a nearby wall, and instead of the roughness of brick, felt a smooth, cool polished surface. Bone. Under her feet, the pavement was of smooth bone.

The cars passing seemed like cars until a more careful look revealed them to be coffins. The buses, when studied, were smooth and white and polished, with fluted columns and pediments, like moving mausoleums.

At the bus-stops stood people in dark clothes, standing still and silent, staring at nothing. People shuffled in and out of the shops that lined the street, but when she looked into the shops, there was nothing for sale.

This was the land of the dead. It hadn't been like this on previous visits. It might not be like this if she came again. Like all places, it changed. She cupped her hands around her mouth and shouted, "Cat! Cat!" Turning, she shouted again, in another direction. None of the passers-by looked at her. None seemed to hear her.

She turned, meaning to call again, but saw, bounding towards her, a large cat, heavy of body and round of head. Its staring eyes were big and green; its ears were tufted at the ends. Bounding up to her, it pressed its big head against her side, and raised a large, soft paw with long, sheathed claws.

Beckerdyke knelt and hugged the big head to her, stroked the tufted ears. "Search," she said, "for the smell of blood – this one died bloodily." Hugging the big cat tighter, she formed in her mind the photograph of Gary she'd seen, and held it, knowing it would pass to the cat-spirit. She thought of the tattoos on his arms: she thought of the girl, Zoe.

"He's new dead, this one, within the year." She opened her arms, releasing the cat. "Go and find him!"

The cat butted her with its head, then turned and bounded away down the streets of bone.

Beckerdyke sat on the smooth, hard pavement. Grey people trudged past her, not noticing her. Coffin-cars and mausoleum-buses ground along the roads. Her next task was to take the bag from her back and prepare for the dead that the cat-spirit would bring back. With the chalks she would draw a circle to protect herself from them. With the bowl and knife she would be ready to feed them so they would talk to her ... but it was too much. She was too tired.

Let Cat search... It would make finding the spirit she needed easier, another day.

Whisking into the air like a leaf, she flew...

And woke in her armchair, in the dark of her room. The gas-fire was on, but she was cold. For a while she thought about fetching the electric fire, but was too weak to make the effort...

But she still had the talent. If the girl came back, she could show her what a real witch could do...

5
WITCH JOURNEY

Duncan was wandering down Saint Etheldreda Street, and had just passed the little local shop with the newspaper placard standing on the pavement outside – LOCAL MAN STABBED IN DRUGS DEAL – when he looked up and saw her. She was on the other side of the street. Her blonde head, with its pony-tail fastened high on its crown and the ringlets cascading down, was bobbing above the roofs of the parked cars.

He stopped, hands in pockets. The girl was staring straight ahead, walking quickly and determinedly, and he had a chance to take a good look at her. There was no doubt it was the girl he was looking for. The olive skin, and the too blonde hair, the monkeyish but very pretty little face. At last!

Of course he'd found her. He'd known he would. It was both amazing and ordinary at the same time. He had been meant to find her, just as he'd been meant to run across her the week before, when she'd been crying in the park. With so many people in the city, all criss-crossing to and fro every day, it was staggering that he should find just one again – but God could do anything, God could make the lame walk and the blind see, so what was strange about it?

Every day since he'd last seen her he'd walked the streets round the park – all of the streets. Up and down, past the terraced houses and the parked cars; up and down the High Street and Shire Oak Road, past the supermarket and the big greengrocers whose sign boasted that it supplied the city's hospitals, past all the little shops and Woolworths and Boots and the Catholic church, and so back into the streets of houses again. Up and down, round and round.

He'd sat on garden walls to rest. He'd eaten by the playground where kids zoomed up and down concrete ramps on skateboards and roller-skates. Eventually he was going to spot her, he knew that. It was just a matter of time, of keeping faith, of being ready when the Lord acted.

And there she was, walking down the street.

"Thank you," he said to God. "Thank you Lord, thank you, thank you." And he ran across the road to meet her.

"Hi! Remember me?"

Zoe was startled and a little alarmed by the shape looming suddenly in front of her, the voice rapping at her. She stepped back to get a better view. A man – a boy – quite young, dressed in a big, baggy parka. His face, thin and pleasant, with dark, shaggy hair, seemed familiar, but she couldn't place him. Probably she'd met him in some pub or club, and he fancied his chance. She gave him a cool, hard stare, to let him know that she didn't remember him, and didn't want to.

"You beat me up the other night."

She remembered the light of the streetlamps being dappled and broken by the trees, and the sound of her own frightened breathing and her scuffling shoes... Abruptly she turned her face away from him and passed him by, involuntarily hunching her shoulders as she did so, afraid he would hit her. "Piss off!"

He walked with her. "I'm glad I found you. It's important."

She stopped and faced him, glaring. "Go *away*!"

He blinked and backed off a pace or two, in no doubt that she really wanted him to go away. But he said, "No, listen…"

She ran away from him, her shoes clacking on

the pavement, her rucksack swinging from one shoulder.

For a moment, Duncan let her go. She was so obviously frightened of him, and he didn't want to frighten her… But in a second, he realized that she was in too much danger for him to just stand and watch her run away. He *had* to talk to her.

Zoe reached Mrs Beckerdyke's house, went in at the gate and spun round in the tiny front yard to push the gate shut as the boy arrived at it. "Bugger off!"

"Is this where the witch lives?" Duncan asked. "Are you going to see her now?" *Oh God*, he thought, *You are great*. Not only had he been brought together with the girl again, but at the very moment when she needed him most. He *had* to save her.

"NONE of your business!"

"It *is* my business. You don't know yet, but it is, it really is." He tried to push the gate open, but her small hands were grasping its top rail and she fiercely shoved it closed again. "You've got to listen," he said.

"Go away and leave me alone or I shall call the police."

"That woman can't help you, whatever you think. She's going to put you in danger, she's—"

"I shall knock on the door if you don't go away, and Mrs Beckerdyke'll phone the police. This is harassment! I'll have you locked up!"

"I'm trying to help you! I'm trying to save you! Why won't you listen?"

Zoe let go of the gate, took the two steps to the door, and knocked and banged on the glass panel. She even kicked the door's lower frame.

Duncan pushed open the gate, but hesitated to go into the yard. "Listen. Calm down. Listen, I've got to tell you this. If your witch calls anything up, it won't be your boyfriend, it won't be anything human, or that ever was –"

She wasn't listening to him. Pointing at his feet, at where his trainers were planted at the edge of the moss-grown flagstones, she said, "That's private. You come on there, you're breaking the law. Mrs Beckerdyke can have the police on you – and her will! Clear off, go on, just clear off!"

Behind her, the door opened. Standing in the doorway was Mrs Beckerdyke, the witch.

Duncan stared. He'd never seen a witch before. She was a tall woman, a tall, broad-shouldered, big woman. Her dark hair, all striped and speckled with grey, was pulled back and tied untidily behind her head. Strands of it curled down about her face and shoulders. Her clothes – she wore a limp old brown cardigan over a dark dress – were untidy and sad. She looked ill: pale, with heavy, bleary eyes. The features of her face were some-how blurred and smudged. She hugged her cardigan around her as if she was cold.

Duncan supposed that, if you were a witch and lived without God, you would be sick. How could you resist all the germs and illnesses and sicknesses that floated around trying to get at you? Before God had come to him, he'd been sick.

"What are you doing," asked the witch, "fighting on my doorstep? What's wrong with you, girl?"

Zoe pointed dramatically at Duncan, snapping her arm out straight and extending it and her finger to their full length. "It's him. He started it. He keeps following me and he won't go away when I tell him."

The witch didn't speak. She simply lifted her large, round-lidded eyes and looked over Zoe's head at him.

Duncan felt the hair over his brow lift slightly as her gaze struck him, and he was impressed with her power. "I ... I need to ... speak to her," he said to Mrs Beckerdyke.

"Tell him to go away!" Zoe said, and grinned maliciously at Duncan, eager to see him cut down to size.

"I shall do no such thing," said Mrs Beckerdyke. "Why don't you simply listen to what he has to say? Then he'll go away happy, and we can get on with our business."

"I'm not talking to him," Zoe said. "He's a nutter. Tell him to sod off."

Elizabeth Beckerdyke settled herself heavily

against her doorpost, her arms still folded. "You must excuse her, she's missing her young man," she said to Duncan. "He was killed, in a car crash. So that's how it is."

"I know," Duncan said. "And…" He tried to find ways of being polite, but then decided to get what he had to say said. God was on his side. There was no need to be shy or embarrassed. "I know why she's come to you. I know what you're going to do." He turned to Zoe. "It's dangerous. You don't know what – what you're opening yourself up to, playing about at this sort of thing. Come away now." He held out his hand. "Come with me."

Zoe wrinkled up her nose and mouth and said, "Bugger off!"

"We'll go to the church, up there," Duncan said. It wasn't a true church, but just one of those poncey, establishment churches – Church of England or Catholic or something, all stained glass and candlesticks and insincerity like that – but at least it was a church, a haven of sorts. "I'll tell you about Jesus. He loves you. That's what you need—"

"Get off, you nutter," Zoe said.

"He knows you're in pain. He'll help. He loves you. Don't get mixed up with her, don't—"

Elizabeth Beckerdyke laughed, and both Duncan and Zoe looked at her.

"You've got a little Christian knight," she said to Zoe. "A little Saint George. Or should that be Saint Andrew? Come to kill the dragon anyway." She lifted her head, opened her mouth wide and gave a loud, deep laugh that carried across the street. "Pity he seems to have mislaid his white charger. Never mind. Why don't you come in, Saint Andrew, and pray for us both? Keep the forces of evil at bay."

Duncan hadn't known what to expect from a witch – hatred, anger perhaps, maybe physical attack – but it hadn't been this gently amused and indulgent tone.

"I don't want him coming in!" Zoe said, while he still stood astonished. She was furious at the intrusion. In fear, and hope, she had imagined herself and Elizabeth Beckerdyke performing some rite… Lighting candles, chanting… Maybe even killing something, if that was what it took. She imagined the spell working, and Gary stepping out of fire with his arms opening… If it worked, then she didn't want some interloper standing by and gawping. If it didn't work – and sometimes she hoped it wouldn't – then she didn't want some stranger there to laugh. "Tell him to sling his hook! Clear off, you—"

"My girl, what you want or don't want is irrelevant," said the witch. "This is my house. I'll invite into it whom I please, without any comment from you." As Zoe's mouth opened, she added,

"And if you want me to do this thing for you, you'll keep your mouth shut." She stood aside, to leave the doorway clear, and asked Duncan, "Are you coming in?"

Although he stood in Saint Etheldreda Street, in Bearwood in Birmingham, in daylight, with cars passing by on the road behind him, and hamburger wrappers blowing in the wind, Duncan had the sudden impression that he was about to take a step in blind darkness – a step that might cost him his balance and throw him into the pit.

It was only a middle-aged woman inviting him into her poky little house for a cup of tea... But he knew that was only what his eyes saw. He had deeper senses, and they were all jangling with warning.

Physically, he was quite safe. It wasn't a matter of a bleeding, swollen lip, or a black eye. It was the very centre of him that was threatened, the part of himself that he called "I". If he stepped in through that door, that "I" could be stifled.

He could turn round and step back through the scabby little gate, as both women wanted him to do, and he could walk away down the street with litter blowing about his legs, and he'd be safe.

But then what? Was he going to go back to the church and praise the God he'd failed again?

"All right," he said, his voice gruff and breathless. As he moved forward, into the house, his arms and legs felt made of concrete, so awkward and heavy were they to move. The little front room was dim, and chilly, as if evil were already closing round him.

Elizabeth Beckerdyke, moving slowly, led the way into her sitting room. Duncan hung back, glancing round the room he found himself in. The curtains were drawn at the windows – that was why it was so dim. There was a table, and a sofa, but both were piled with books, magazines, piles of washing and other oddments. It obviously wasn't used much.

Zoe, glowering, shoved past him and followed Beckerdyke through into the other room. Duncan's heart had begun to quicken its beat with big, heavy thuds. Feeling as if he was moving a tremendous weight with every step, he made himself follow.

A tiny, dark hallway brought him into another small room, where the air was so hot, it was like walking into a thick mass of cotton-wool. The curtains were drawn in this room too, and the electric light gave a flat, yellowish cast to everything.

Elizabeth Beckerdyke had seated herself in an armchair, and had her feet propped on a white coffee table. Zoe as standing in front of her, in the middle of the room. Both of them stared at Duncan.

"Shut the door," Beckerdyke said. "I'm cold."

He was reluctant to shut himself into the small room with them. As he slowly reached out a hand to obey, he was looking round, expecting to see some signs of Satanism or witchcraft. Images jangled in his head: human skulls and black cockerels bleeding, their heads ripped off; candles and pentagrams and inverted crucifixes.

There was nothing like that. A large computer screen occupied the alcove beside the fireplace, and there was a small television on the floor. Newspapers lay everywhere, scattered and in piles. Books were stacked beside the fireplace. A small and very old-fashioned cassette-player stood on the table.

He pulled the door shut. Immediately, the room became so hot that he broke into a sweat.

"A Christian," said the witch. She was studying him with a calm interest. "I was a Christian once."

Duncan blinked. He hadn't known – he didn't believe – that a witch could ever have been a Christian.

"Oh, yes," the witch said, nodding. "I was raised a Christian. Church every Sunday. But Christianity makes no sense."

Nettled, Duncan said, "It makes sense to me."

The witch smiled. "What's your name?"

Duncan opened his mouth to answer, but then held his breath. Instinctively, he felt it would be dangerous to tell her his real name.

Zoe had been fidgeting, pacing the length of the sofa and back. "Never mind him! What about me?"

The witch didn't even look at her, just said, "Be quiet. Or go away."

Zoe made a short, angry exclamation, and threw herself down on the sofa.

To Duncan, Beckerdyke said, "Are you afraid of me? Do you think I'm more powerful than your God?"

"I'm Duncan Selby."

The witch held out her hand. "Pleased to meet you, Duncan. Elizabeth Beckerdyke."

Duncan almost jumped across the room to shake her hand, determined not to let her think he was afraid of her – though he was – or that his faith in Christ was weak. Her hand was thick, fleshy, but rather damp and cool. They shook hands but when he tried to withdraw his, she held on to it. "I believe in Christ too," she said.

He stared at her.

"But I would call him Freyr, or Woden, or Adonis or Tammuz." She shrugged. "Osiris. There are hundreds of these corn-gods, who die every autumn and rise again in the spring." She saw the puzzlement in Duncan's face, and said, "Of course, Christ's story has become garbled, but he's a corn-god like all the rest – and they all embody the 'good' side of life – or what people like to think of as the 'good' side. Spring and summer, warmth, light, growth, life –"

Zoe, sprawled on the sofa with her arms and legs crossed, gave a loud, exasperated sigh. Duncan glanced at her, but Mrs Beckerdyke ignored her. "Oh aye?" Duncan said, bemused at finding himself being lectured on … on what exactly? The string of strange names meant nothing to him.

"But there's another side of life," Mrs Beckerdyke said. "Isn't there? Cold, dark, disease, death, war, discord –"

"Evil," Duncan said.

"No. Not evil. That's too simplistic. There has to be death and decay, so there can be renewal and growth. Don't you see that?"

Duncan shook his head.

Mrs Beckerdyke smiled, a rather kindly smile, as if she felt sorry for his lack of understanding. "What you call 'evil' is a power just as great and just as necessary as 'good' – and as worthy of worship. Set. Loki. Hecate. Hel. You'll never understand this world by trying to think of them simply as 'evil'." Beckerdyke waved a hand. "The work of the Devil. Nothing to do with us, who are *good*. That's like peering at the world through a tiny peephole, but pretending to yourself that you can see everything.

"*Hello*," Zoe said, and kicked the sofa. "Remember me?"

"That's why I moved on from the simplicities, the naiveties of Christianity," Beckerdyke said, still looking at Duncan. "I daresay you will, in time."

"No," Duncan said. He hadn't followed everything she'd said, but the gist of it seemed to be exactly what someone working for evil – a witch – *would* say.

The witch laughed again, shaking her head, and then looked across the room at Zoe. "You, madam. Do you still want this? Are you sure?"

"Not with him here," Zoe said.

"I want him here," Beckerdyke said. "I sense promise in Duncan. And I need an apprentice." She laughed again, more softly this time, and then sat back in her chair, spreading her hands on the arms. "I'm ready." She nodded towards the table and the cassette-player. "Put that on."

From where she sat on the sofa, Zoe looked up at Duncan, as if expecting him to obey. When he didn't move, she tutted and got up, glowering at him, and went over to the table. She studied the cassette-player for a moment, and then pressed the "play" button. They heard the creaking as the old machine turned the tape, and then loud, fast rhythmic drumming started, its sound thin and scratchy.

Beckerdyke leaned back in her chair even more, closing her eyes.

Duncan stepped to the table, and pressed the cassette button, releasing it. The drumming stopped. "I can't let you do this. You can't –"

"I'm flying," Beckerdyke said. "I'm going. I'm on my way."

Though the woman was a metre away, in her armchair, her voice echoed, as if she shouted and her words carried from a distance. Startled, Duncan remained at the table, his hand hovering above the cassette-player.

"Over the earth I go!" Beckerdyke was smiling. Happy tears ran down her cheeks. She was starving and light-headed, her body weak and cold, and at the first sound of the drum, her spirit had slipped loose and flown from her with delicious ease. Now she felt the air brushing her skin and tugging at her hair; it whooped past her ears. Below, wheeling by, she saw the green earth and the grey, white-flecked sea. Round about her in the air, birds buoyed and screamed... And there, below, was the hill, the green hill, with the graves climbing up it and the brambles growing over the stones. She swooped towards it.

Duncan was still by the table. Zoe hadn't moved either, but, though she disliked the Scots boy, the room was small and she had either to stay near the boy or move closer to the witch.

Beckerdyke raised her arms above her head. "Under the earth I go!" The cry was so loud, and the gesture so sudden, that both Zoe and Duncan started. With a flinch, Duncan turned his head to look into the corners of the room behind him.

Into the grave Beckerdyke dived, joyfully swallowing the earth, breasting through the cold clay, swimming through it.

Zoe slipped around the table, its hard edge digging into her hip, until she was in the corner beside it, further from the witch. Willing the witch on, she whispered, "Under the earth go!" She didn't know she'd spoken. She didn't know that her knees were bending, taking her into a half-crouch. Her fists were clenched, digging her nails into her palms. She didn't feel it.

Duncan's hands gripped the table behind him. There's nothing to be afraid of here, he told himself. A silly woman, play-acting, trying to seem important. And such an ordinary little room. The hearth-rug was frayed at the edges, and long, tangled strands of material trailed across the thin carpet. The small electric fire's two bars burned cherry red. The curtains, with their ugly pattern of big flowers, hung limply at the windows. The three cheap doors – one into the hall, one into the kitchen and one opening on the steep stairs – had grubby paintwork marked and smeared by fingers. Devil-worship, black magic, surely didn't happen in such down-at-heel little rooms.

In the armchair the sick-looking woman

slumped, her feet sprawled before her on the coffee-table, her head rolling against the chair's back. Her arms lifted in the air, with spread fingers or clawed hands – or they dropped, limply, to hang over the chair's arms.

"I'm climbing now... Struggling through... Struggling out..." That voice wasn't coming from inside the room or from anywhere near them. "This is the Land of the Dead." It was all the cold grey of concrete by moonlight, and the darkness of black, unreflecting panes of glass. "The dead stand and stare, they stare at me and stare and bone is under my feet... And now I'll search. Now I'll call."

An extraordinary sound came from the witch's mouth – an ululating shriek, a caterwaul. Both Zoe and Duncan jumped. Zoe sank right down to her knees on the floor. Duncan's head snatched round, startled by her sudden disappearance below the level of the table. He felt a pang of fright and loneliness, as if he'd been deserted.

"Please, please," Zoe was whispering to herself. "Please, please, please..."

In the Land of the Dead, Beckerdyke prepared for her work. From the bag she carried with her, she took a pack of chalks. Choosing the green chalk, she drew a wide circle on the bone-white pavement. Her hands strayed, and the circle wasn't true, but it didn't matter because, in this dream-time, it sprang back into shape.

Beckerdyke stepped into the circle, knelt, and took from her bag a shallow bowl – a little blue and white cereal dish – and a sharp knife. She looked up and saw, pacing towards her through the lampposts made of bones, the Cat. Behind it straggled a small group of grey figures. "Have you found the one I need?" she called out. "Have you brought him?"

The Cat entered the green circle and sat by Beckerdyke's side. The ghosts crowded about the circle's edge. Getting to her feet, Beckerdyke walked about the circle, looking at them, remembering the photographs she'd seen of the young man before he was killed. There was one ghost who was certainly not any wraith of him. "Go away," she said, making a motion of her hand, as if to push the thing away. It fell back, like an eddying of smoke, away from the circle's edge.

But the others – were they what remained of the one she looked for, or not? Her memory was not so sharp, nor had the photographs been so clear, that she could say for certain. They might be, they might not.

Beckerdyke returned to the circle's centre, where she knelt beside the bowl and picked up the knife. She drew the sharp blade twice across her forearm. The pain was a brief, bright sting, and then the blood ran down in streams. She held her arm above the bowl, so that the blood ran into it.

When the bowl was full she picked it up, stood, and faced the ghosts again. Smelling the blood, they jostled forward eagerly.

"Who wants to drink?" she asked, and offered the blood to the nearest, holding the bowl while it drank. When it raised its head, its mouth was bloodied, and its face was taking on colour. Beckerdyke gave it her hand and drew it over the chalk line into the circle. There was a ripple of movement as all the others pressed close, but the chalk line held them back as if it had been a fence.

Beckerdyke looked over at the Cat, but it was couched in its fur, its eyes closed, unperturbed by the ghost. "Speak up now!" Beckerdyke said. "Tell me your name."

The ghost opened its bloodied lips and mouthed, but made no sound.

"No lies now! What is your name?"

The ghost mouthed and choked, making noises, but nothing that she wanted to hear. "Go away," Beckerdyke said. "You're not the one." The ghost shrank back, and darted from the circle as if yanked by a tether.

Beckerdyke returned to the circle's edge, and offered the bowl of her own blood to the next ghost. The cat blinked and flicked one ear as this ghost entered the circle, but otherwise did not stir. But this ghost could not give the answers she wished to hear either, and she dismissed it.

As she did the next, and the next, and the next. Then there was only one ghost to be offered the blood. It drank from the offered bowl and stepped into the circle. At once the Cat opened its eyes and got to its feet. The fur rose on its back, and it hissed. Beckerdyke saw, but still she said to the ghost, "Tell me your name!"

Duncan and Zoe listened miserably as Beckerdyke cried out again, arching her back so that her upper body touched the armchair only at the crown of her head. Her voice rose and fell, uttering a long stream of words. It seemed to plead, then to order or mock – but not one word of it could they understand.

A foreign language, Duncan thought; and for a few seconds tried to guess what it was. It didn't have the sound of German or French – was it Welsh? And then he realized, with a sick jolt, that it wasn't any human language at all. The witch's voice ululated and trilled strangely, rising up the scale to a nerve-scratching wail, or shrinking abruptly to a note lower than a man's. She was talking to something, in that other place from which her voice carried, but whatever she was questioning or mocking might not even be human.

He looked into the corners again, to check that they were still uninhabited, and said, "Our Father, which art in Heaven … deliver us from evil, deliver us from evil. Deliver us… Amen."

Zoe knelt, both hands pressed over her mouth. The images in her mind see-sawed between Gary as she remembered him – solid and warm and loving – and Gary as she feared he might now be – pallid and oozing, stinking, full of maggots. See-sawing between longing and repulsion, she drove her nails into her face, and waited, and forgot to draw breath.

When the ghost looked into her face but didn't answer, Beckerdyke said, "In Woden's name, in Hermes' name, answer me!"

"I am Zoe's man." There was nothing strange about the voice, but the Cat spat and prowled an arc of the circle, its tail bristling.

"Tell me no lies now! In Woden's name, who were you?"

"Zoe's man."

Beckerdyke seized the cold face in her hand and raised the head. The eyes met hers, and she saw a bright gleam in them quickly die, as they became dead and filmed. "You lie," she said. "You never were human."

"I was Zoe's man."

The Cat growled, and Beckerdyke raised her hand to dismiss the thing. It was a spirit, but not the spirit of Zoe's friend, or of any other man. Perhaps it was simply a spirit out of place, the spirit of an animal, tree or stone that mischievously wanted to try life as a man. Perhaps it was one of the spirits of disease, or madness that wanted to find a way into the human world.

Again Beckerdyke raised her hand to dismiss the thing, but stopped. The Cat, her helper, had gone out and gathered these spirits, and she had rejected all but this one. The ghost she searched for, the ghost of Zoe's young man, was not to be found – it had drifted beyond, into another of the many worlds. If she dismissed this spirit, she would return to her own world a failure. How that girl, the little guttersnipe, would jeer.

She dipped her fingers in the bowl of blood, and wrote her name on the spirit's forehead. "In my name, I bind you to me." She wrote her name first on the spirit's right cheek, then on its left. "In Woden's name I bind you to my command." She would take the spirit back and only after the girl and the Scots boy had been impressed would she dismiss it.

Taking both the spirit's hands in hers, she said, "Come with me. Back to the sky I go!"

The hair moved above Duncan's brow. The voice was coming back towards them, approaching from a distance, coming back between the walls.

The tension left Beckerdyke's body and she slumped back. Her head turned from side to side against the chair's headrest. "Over the earth we come! We come, we come!"

Into the room came – Duncan felt the touch of it – something cold. It was more solid than a draught; it nudged against him, heavy, insistent, but invisible and silent.

"We come, we come!"

It was as bitingly cold as iron on a freezing day. Duncan's flesh recoiled from it, moving on his bones. Into his nose and the back of his mouth crept a metallic stink, a taste as if he'd bitten into something rotten.

His vision was vivid in his mind: the grey army, fish-bellied and slug-bodied, the evil things –

"We come!" the witch cried, "We come!"

"Amen, amen, amen," Duncan said. "Our Father. Deliver us from evil."

There was a shimmer in the air at the centre of the room, like the heat-shimmer seen above roads on a hot summer day. The bending of the air distorted and twisted the straight lines of chimney-breast, mantelpiece and gas-fire.

Duncan shook his head, to deny what he saw. "Deliver us from evil, deliver us –"

Zoe, on her knees, slid her face down into her hands so that her eyes were covered. She was shivering with little, constant shivers, as if it was a cold day and her clothes were too thin.

Something appeared in the heat-shimmer at the centre of the room, something that was glimpsed, and then sparkled apart, or sank, before it could be recognized – like a broken reflection in rippling water.

"Make way!" cried the witch. "Stand aside! We are here!"

The broken reflection was settling… A broad, meaty young man emerged from it. He was naked, a little paunchy, but the wide, rounded face under the close-cropped hair was grinning.

The ghost didn't look evil. It looked mundane. But Duncan could feel the stinking cold reaching from it – the air around him, touching his skin, so cold that it burned; and he felt a stink reaching down into his throat, so rancid that he retched. He held his breath and couldn't pray, expect in his mind. He stared at the thing fixedly, stared until his eyes hurt, and repeated in his mind: *Our Father, Our Father, Our Father…*

The ghost's lips moved. It said, barely above a breath, "Zo?"

Zoe heard her name spoken in a voice she knew. It was a voice so familiar, speaking in so well-known and affectionate a tone, that she forgot all fear. She took her hands from her face and lifted her head.

There was Gary, grinning at her, just as she remembered him. Looking at his solid, meaty body with its broad, hairy chest and rounded belly, she rose from her knees, knowing just how solid he would feel when she put her arms round him. She bent up one knee, getting her feet under her, ready to stand. All the time, she never took her eyes from Gary, anticipating how warm he would be as she slipped her arms round him, how her head would notch into the hollow of his shoulder and how, as his smell rose into her nose, his hand would fit the round at the back of her head.

Duncan watched Zoe getting up and couldn't believe that she was going to the thing, with its cold and its stink. Without thinking, he reached for her, meaning to catch hold of her and drag her back, but it was as if he tried to move against a concrete wall, as if he was pressed against a wall and trying to push his way through it. He said, "God." The word creaked out of him, and he despaired. But then heat flickered and licked round him: strong, dry heat, like the touch of the tropical sun. It sank into him, glowed in his bones, wrapped him round, so he felt the heat and weight of it, like a heavy mantle. The wall that had held him back melted before the heat and he lunged, almost fell, forward.

Gary reached out his hand to Zoe as she rose, his eyes crinkling in a smile. She reached out her hand to him.

Duncan shoved between them, knocking her hand aside. His touch was like the end of a lighted cigarette, and she snatched herself away, startled and burned.

94

Duncan was assailed, shaken, withered. He was like a candle-flame blown, torn and almost doused by a strong, icy wind. Inwardly and outwardly, he quailed. His mind, his very self, guttered, wavered and he looked into more than darkness, into a deeper, vaster and greater desolation than oblivion. He glimpsed hell. Then – such unearthly relief – the warmth around him flared and grew. He was at its centre, still whole, still alive. And, more than that, still *himself*.

Zoe, recovering from the shock of the Scots boy's burning touch, looked round and saw that Gary was gone.

She was in a hot, shabby little room, with a cold draught blowing through it from the open door. A woman snored in an armchair, her feet propped gracelessly on a coffee-table. The Scots boy stood, gawping, in front of her.

Zoe shoved past him, to embrace the empty air where Gary had been. Having nothing to hold, and nothing to hold her up, she sank to the hearth-rug. There she lay. She wanted to see nothing, hear nothing, know nothing. Her face crumpled in pain, but she made no sound. She had no tears.

Duncan put his hands to his face, and felt tears on his fingers. He was shaking, and felt so weak he could hardly stand. His blood was still chilled, and though the terrible stink that had filled the room was gone, it lingered in his nose and sickened him. Zoe lay at his feet, the Beckerdyke woman sprawled in the armchair, but he couldn't help them yet. He had to stumble through into the kitchen and throw up in the sink.

Despite all, he could feel the love around him. Despite the retching and the shuddering, he could feel the love pressing down on him like a heavy blanket on his head and shoulders. He had prayed, and Christ had answered. Christ was great; Christ was Love.

He gulped water from the tap and wiped his mouth on his sleeve.

Now he had to help the two women.

6

ZOE

Duncan stood in the doorway of the kitchen and looked from the woman slumped in the armchair to the girl lying on the floor. He didn't know what to do.

He still shook with revulsion and fear and, far from looking after someone else, felt he needed someone to look after him. That, of course, wasn't possible. No one cuddled big lads because they were afraid. People just laughed instead.

He thought of phoning for the police or an ambulance, and then just walking out of the door and away, so he wouldn't have to cope with any of this.

But he was here, on the spot. He should do something. Jesus would have done.

That woman had called the thing here: the loathsome thing that had nearly blown him out. If he went near her, if he touched her, he might stir something up. It might come back.

He had to do it. If he wanted to call himself a Christian. If he wanted to call himself brave.

The woman was snoring, so at least she was breathing. That let him go to the girl first, though he was careful not to turn his back on the woman. Crouching beside the girl, he reached tentatively to touch her shoulder. She twisted and lashed out at him with her fist. "Bastard!"

He moved away from her, and went to stand beside the woman in the armchair. Beckerdyke's feet were splayed on the coffee table, her head rested on her shoulder, and she dribbled.

It took him some minutes before he could make himself touch her hand. He was so afraid of bringing back the ghost and its presence. But he did it, and her hand was warm. There couldn't be much wrong with her, then. Probably all that was needed was that she be kept warm until she woke up. He crossed the room to the door that opened on to the steep stairs, and looked up into that narrow, dark space. He was nervous about going up there. A light switch was beside the door, and he snapped it on, lighting the stairwell with a dingy yellow light. A cold draught blew down it.

"God be with me," he said, and scrambled up the steps.

Zoe pushed with her arms and sat up. Her head still hung, too heavy to lift. She considered making the effort of getting herself to her feet and getting herself home.

And then getting up the next day. And getting through the day. Only to have to get up the next day, and get through that day, and the next, and the next, and the next, all the time knowing that she was never going to see Gary again in this life. That he was gone, and she could never have him back. Not in this life. Never in this life. She hadn't understood the meaning of "never" before. Now she knew it to be the cruelest, emptiest word in the language. Never. Never, Never.

It'll get better with time, her mother said. You'll get over it, her gran said. He's gone to a better place. We'll all be united when the Lord calls us.

Zoe didn't believe, as her gran did, in a happy-ever-after, where a kindly God gathered together all friends and loved ones, and let them drift about for eternity in a shining rose-garden. Life wasn't like that. Why should the afterlife be?

God would keep her from Gary, just to spite her. They'd both be going to hell, wouldn't they? Both of them had told lies, and stolen things, and had lusted, and been angry and proud and slothful and all the rest. You couldn't be alive without doing all those things, but God punished you for them anyway. So they'd both be in hell but, because it was hell, they wouldn't be allowed to be together.

If she was ever going to be with Gary again, it wouldn't be with God's help.

Zoe couldn't stand it. She couldn't stand it *now*. It hurt too much. She couldn't live like this for another endless year. And she might live for another sixty years before she died. Sixty years of this!

She shook her head, and got to her feet slowly, as if she was seventy rather than seventeen. Catching hold of her rucksack's strap, she hauled it with her into the kitchen, and from the kitchen through a short, dark passage into the bare, cold bathroom, with its white bath and basin, its white lavatory and white walls.

Sitting on the hard, narrow rim of the bath, she delved into her rucksack, and brought out a plastic drum of paracetamol. It was a bigger drum than you could buy now, holding more tablets. It had been in her gran's kitchen cupboard for years, but there was still a layer of pills on the bottom. Opening the drum, she shook out a handful of tablets, and then looked round. How was she to take them?

Tipping the tablets back into their drum, she

wandered back into the kitchen. The stainless steel draining board beside the sink was stacked with saucepans and crockery, but no cups. Turning her head, she saw a row of mugs hanging on hooks at the back of the dresser.

She took one down, and filled it with water at the sink. Among the things on the draining board she noticed a large knife. It was almost a cleaver, and it looked sharp. Clumsily, with the hand that already clutched the drum of tablets, she picked up the knife, and went back into the bathroom.

She sat on the edge of the bath again, and put the knife into the hand-basin.

Once more she opened the drum of tablets and looked inside it. White tablets jumbled together in a white drum. She asked herself: do I want to do this?

But then, do I want to wake up tomorrow?

Not if it was going to be like today. Not if it was going to hold more disappointments like today.

A little courage, and she could be with Gary again. Or, if not with him, at least in the same place he was. Which would be something. Not much, but something.

She tipped four tablets into her palm, tossed them into her mouth and gulped them down with a mouthful of water.

Too slow. She put the plastic drum to her lips and filled her mouth with tablets. There were too many to swallow, so she crunched them between her teeth, and they tasted foul and made her shudder, especially when she drank and swallowed. But she could put up with a bad taste for a little while. She could put up with almost anything if it meant getting back to Gary. Or just ending.

There were no more tablets. Slipping from the edge of the bath, she sat on the floor in the narrow space between the bath and the wall, her legs folded up against her chest. She waited for something to happen, imagining that everything might start going dark, or wobbly. Her sight remained just as clear and steady as before. The only thing she felt was slightly sick, from taking large gulps of cold water and nasty-tasting tablets. Her heart raced too, in a strange way that made her body feel insubstantial and hollow, but that was probably just fear.

Coward, she said to herself. Why be scared? Living is what you ought to be scared of.

She looked at the knife in the basin. She'd been hoping she wouldn't have to use it. But if it would get her out of this. All it needed was a little courage.

She stood up, using the edge of the bath to help her, and was surprised when she swayed a little. Her head was light, spinning, and she staggered as she took the step closer to the basin.

The handle of the knife was big and solid, but

her hand didn't find it as solid as her eyes told her she would. She held the knife up in her right hand, and stretched out her left wrist. Go for it, she told herself…

Duncan came awkwardly down the steep stairs with a duvet bundled up in his arms. The empty, jumble-filled rooms he'd found upstairs had been cold and sad, but free of the presence he feared. The one room furnished sparsely as a bedroom had been even sadder, but simply lonely, that was all. The carpet on the floor had been dirty and torn, the wardrobe a tall, dark-brown, old-fashioned thing that looked as if it had come from a junk-shop. A single bed in one corner had been heaped with a tangled duvet without a cover, the pillowcase had been grubby, stained where a head had lain, and the sheet had been dragged back to show the dusty mattress. The only other things in the room had been a rickety old kitchen chair, and some card-board boxes full of books. It had reminded Duncan of the rooms in the hostel where he stayed: temporary camping places, uncomfortable and makeshift. He hadn't imagined that anyone with their own home would live in such a way. For a moment he'd stood in the room, feeling almost sorry for the witch. Then he snatched the duvet from the bed and hurried back downstairs.

At every step, folds of the duvet had threatened

to get under his feet and trip him, and he kept pausing to bunch it more tightly; but he reached the bottom safely and kicked the stair-door open. The witch was still sleeping in her chair. The girl had gone.

Duncan threw the duvet over the sleeping woman, who drew her head back sharply as it flapped in her face. She gasped, snorted, and slept again. Once he was sure she wasn't going to wake, Duncan turned to look for the girl.

The door to the front room was still closed – but he noticed that her rucksack was gone. Maybe she'd left the house, closing the door after her. But the door leading the other way, into the kitchen, was standing open.

He went through it. The girl wasn't in the kitchen, and he thought, again, that she must have left – but then he heard a clatter from the bathroom. So that was where she was. He withdrew into the living room, sat on the sofa and watched Mrs Beckerdyke sleep.

He was unhappy about being there. He felt like an intruder. The woman seemed pretty out of it. What if she woke up, forgot that she'd invited him in, and started screaming? The last thing he needed was for the police to be called. Where do you live? they'd ask. They thought anybody who didn't have a permanent address was some kind of crook.

He thought again about leaving … but the woman was unconscious. Someone ought to stay and keep an eye on her. Then there was the girl. She was upset, and someone ought to stay around and make sure she was all right.

Mrs Beckerdyke gave a particularly loud snore, which made him look up with a start; and then he realized that the girl was still in the bathroom.

She'd been a long time. And she was very upset.

He stood up.

He ought to check on her, but it was embarrassing. She might be doing something, well, private. Some girl thing. And she didn't like him. If he went and asked her what she was doing, she'd be angry.

But what would Jesus do?

Jesus wouldn't care about embarrassment. He'd check up on her, because it was the right thing to do.

He went into the kitchen. Standing by the door, he could look through the open door on the opposite side of the room, into the little hallway. He could see the bathroom door. It was closed.

He cleared his throat and called, "Excuse me." After waiting a moment, he tried again. "Excuse me. Miss? Are you all right?"

There wasn't a sound from the bathroom.

All of a sudden, he was scared and went quickly through the kitchen and into the little hallway, until he was standing right outside the bathroom door.

The door wasn't locked or even properly closed. It was a smooth white door, slightly too large for its frame, and couldn't be locked because it wouldn't close completely. He could just push the door open and go in. But, somehow, it seemed even ruder to barge in when it would be so easy. He couldn't make himself do it.

Instead, he tapped with one knuckle. "Hello, Miss? Are you in there?" From the other side of the door, silence. Yet he had heard someone moving in there. He was almost certain the girl was in the bathroom. "Are you all right?"

Still there was no answer. He listened hard, his ear to the door, and he couldn't hear any movement at all, not even a sigh or a breath.

"Listen, if you don't answer me, I'm coming in. Hear? I'm coming in. Last chance: are you all right?"

Still no sound.

"Right." He pushed the door open slowly, ready to retreat if she rushed at him, or tried to slam it shut on his head. But there was no resistance. The girl was sitting on the narrow strip of floor between the bath and the wall, her legs folded up to her chest to fit into the space.

"What you doing?" Duncan asked. Even as he was speaking, he registered that she had a knife in her hand. A big kitchen knife, its handle black, its triangular silver blade at least twenty centimetres long. The blade was smeared rustily.

She was holding it in her right hand, and holding her left hand out in front of her. Her left wrist was scored with red lines, and there were red dribbles. There were dark stains on her clothes, and, on the red floor, there were wet, redder patches. The realization hit him like a blow and rocked him on his feet: the wet smears and stains were blood. She had cut her wrist.

"Oh my God!" He spun round, meaning to run into the other room and phone for an ambulance – but stopped the spin halfway, and swung round again. He should try to stop the bleeding before he did anything else.

The girl dropped the knife with a clatter, and Duncan took a step away from her, towards the kitchen. Phone first, to make sure experts were on the way, then see what he could do –

But again he spun, and made a dive towards where she sat on the bathroom floor. She might bleed to death while he was phoning, and he was already wasting time, wasting time –

"Piss off," she said. Her voice was thick and a little slow, as if she'd been drinking. "Leave me alone."

"Shut up!" As he spoke he saw, lying on the floor, the small, round, plastic canister, the kind that pills come in. Its lid was off and it was empty. Snatching his head up to look at the girl's face, he saw specks of crushed white tablet on her lips and at the corners of her mouth. "Oh bloody hell!" he said. "You. You doughnut!"

Dropping to his knees, he grabbed her bleeding hand and pulled it towards him, feeling blood turn sticky on his skin. She tried to pull away, but he held on tightly. "Oh God," he said. The words were merely an exclamation, an automatic expression of shock. But then he heard his own words and they became a prayer. "Oh God, Oh Jesus, help me, help me now, I need Your help…"

"Get off." The girl tried to push him away with her free hand.

He knocked her hand away. "I'm trying to help you." An old green towel hung over the edge of the bath, and he snatched it up.

"I don't want your help, you bastard!" The girl slapped him and scratched at his face, then made a grab for the big knife. He saw what she meant to do, gained it first, and threw it over his shoulder into the little hallway behind him. It clattered on the floor.

The girl shoved him, and pulled away hard, but he grappled with her, struggling to wrap the towel round her bleeding wrist. Pressure. That was what stopped bleeding.

"Leave me alone!" She was crying.

Duncan got a corner of the towel round the girl's small wrist and gripped it in his own larger hand, squeezing hard. As her other hand came at him again, he caught that wrist too, and held it tight. She tried to fight free, but he was bigger and much stronger, and perhaps the tablets she'd taken were having their effect too. Her head ducked towards his hands, and she gnawed at his knuckle. Her teeth scraping on his bone hurt excruciatingly and, letting go of her and snatching his head back, Duncan cuffed her round the head. She burst into louder tears and slumped to the floor.

"Sorry. But you bit me!" He bent low over her, unwrapping the towel. Most of the bleeding had stopped – but there was blood turning thick and sticky on his hands, and blood on his sleeves and the legs of his jeans. "Oh please, Jesus, help her, let her be all right." He hardly knew her, but at that moment it was the most important thing in his life, in the world, that she be all right. What to do, what to do? He had to call for an ambulance but, if he left her here, what would she get up to while he was away? He could take her into the other room, but would moving her be dangerous?

"Come on, up, up you get, up."

He got hold of her under the arms and tried to lift her up, but she wouldn't do anything to help, wouldn't get her feet under her, and her weight slumped suddenly this way and that, pulling him off-balance. She was a small girl, but it was hard work trying to pick her up, especially as he was almost afraid to touch her, worrying about where his hands might go.

But after the third time that she dropped back to the floor and, sweating with the effort and embarrassment, he'd had to pick her up yet again, he stopped bothering about being polite, and bundled her up in his arms like the duvet, and never mind if he had a handful of breast, never mind if her short skirt rode up and showed her knickers. He got her on to her wobbly feet, but her tipsy weight staggered him and they both nearly fell into the bath – as it was, Duncan's leg was pressed painfully into the bath's hard edge.

"Into the other room," he said, breathlessly, and tried to walk her through the doorway into the hall – but the bathroom door swung shut on them, and he had to try and hold her up while he elbowed it open again, and she was swaying about and trying to sit down on the floor. He lugged at her aggressively and they stumbled through into the hallway where Duncan decided to reorganize things. He turned round and walked backwards, dragging the girl after him, which was easier, but still awkward, because she wouldn't help, and tried to pick the knife up from the floor again.

He collected more bruises in the kitchen, as he

manoeuvred the girl's dead weight round the sharp, hard corners of the sink and dresser, and then through the door into the living-room. But, eventually, breathless, he reached the sofa on the far side of the room, and dumped the girl on it.

"Wha...? What?" Elizabeth Beckerdyke started up and stared round at the noise of their entrance, then fell back and slept again.

Duncan stood over the girl for a moment, expecting her to get up and fight, but she just lay there, crying. So he looked round for the phone.

It was lying at his feet, a white one, in long coils of its own cable. When he grabbed up the receiver, the other half fell back to the floor with a crash. He stabbed at the buttons – nine, nine, nine.

"Which service? Fire, Police or Ambulance?"

"Ambulance, I need an ambulance, quick, an overdose – she's cut her wrist—"

"Putting you through."

The phone started ringing again. "Oh come on," Duncan said. "Come on, come on, come on."

The ringing stopped, there was a click, and a voice said, "Ambulance. What's your name, please?"

"I don't know – she's taken an overdose – cut her—"

"What's your name, please, sir?"

"It doesn't matter—"

"Can you give me your name, please, sir?"

He shouted, "Duncan Selby, for God's sake!"

"And your address?"

"I. I don't have. I don't have an address."

"Can you give me the address you're phoning from, please, sir?"

"It's it's – it's Saint Etheldreda Street. I don't know – hang on, hang on."

Still holding the phone, he yanked open the door and ran through into the front room, pulling the long phone-cable as it caught on things and held him back. He opened the street door and looked for the number. To his relief, there was a decorative "15" fastened to the wall.

"Oh thank God! Number fifteen," he said into the phone. "Bearwood. Saint Etheldreda Street. Come quick, please. She's taken an overdose and cut her wrists, please—"

"The ambulance is on its way," said the operator. "It will be with you soon." And she rang off.

Duncan looked up and down the street, but there was no sign of the ambulance. Leaving the door standing open, he ran back inside. Elizabeth Beckerdyke had lifted her head and was looking about blearily. She stared at Duncan in puzzlement, but then appeared to recognize him, and laid her head down on the arm of her chair, pillowed in the crook of her elbow. The girl was still lying on the sofa, whimpering.

Duncan walked to and fro across the narrow

space of the small room. Hearing engine noise from the street, he ran back into the front room and looked out of the door. Still no sign of the ambulance. He went back to the living room and perched on a chair for a moment before jumping up and pacing again. The girl went quiet.

"Are you OK?" he demanded, bending down by her.

"Piss off," she said.

He supposed that meant she was all right, and started pacing again. He said, "Jesus, Jesus, help us, help me, help us all."

Still no ambulance. Should he phone again? He went to look from the front door. Nothing but the narrow street crowded with parked cars. Would the ambulance be able to get along it? He went back to the living room, determined not to look again until – and then the door banged and a man's voice shouted, "Hello? Somebody call for an ambulance?"

Duncan was dizzy with relief. "In here!" Two men in dark blue uniforms came shouldering through the narrow door into the little room, taking up most of the space that was left. "It's her!" Duncan said, pointing to the girl on the sofa. "She cut her wrist and took tablets."

One of the men knelt beside the sofa and said, "How are you, love? Let's have a look." She swore at him and jabbed at him with an elbow. "Now, now, don't be like that."

The other man stood looking at Elizabeth Beckerdyke, who was still hiding her head on the arm of her chair. "D'you know what she took, mate?"

"I... Oh. Hang on." Duncan went clumsily, as fast as he could, through the doorway and through the cramped, narrow space of the kitchen and hallway, into the bathroom. The empty plastic drum still lay on the floor. He picked it up and read the blue lettering on the side. "Paracetamol!" he shouted, and then struggled back through the narrow, awkward house, his path blocked by cardboard boxes holding vegetables, litter-trays and mop handles that fell on him from corners. "It was paracetamol!" he cried, bursting back into the living room.

The man by the sofa was holding the girl's hand and talking quietly to her. The other was stooping over Elizabeth Beckerdyke, but looked up. "D'you know how many there was in it?" He came over and took the empty drum from Duncan, who shook his head. "D'you know how long ago she took 'em?"

"Oh. Ah." Duncan tried to think, but his brain seemed to have jammed. "Not an hour. It hasn't been an hour."

"And how many were in here, d'you know?" The ambulanceman was holding the empty plastic drum.

"I don't know. I didn't know she had it. It was empty when I found it by her side."

The ambulanceman looked unhappy. To his colleague, he said, "I'll get the stretcher," and went out of the door.

The other ambulanceman was sitting on the sofa beside the girl. "What's your name, love?"

"Piss off!"

"Don't be like that. I'm Stan. See, I've told you my name. What's yours?"

"Leave me alone."

"All right. Can you remember how many you took, love? It's important. How many did you take, and how long ago?"

"I want to die," the girl said. "I want to be with him. I want to –"

"No you don't," Stan said. "No you don't, sweetheart, not really. Not tomorrow you won't, you'll see."

Zoe gave a small screech, threw herself face down on the sofa, and beat at it with her fists.

The ambulanceman patted her back. "It'll be all right. It'll be all right."

Duncan found him comforting, and moved closer. "What about the? Her … wrist?"

"Superficial," Stan said, above the girl's head. "A bit of blood'll spread itself about and look like a lot, but her can't have lost much really. Promise you."

The other ambulanceman put his head in from

the hall. "Can't get the stretcher in here. Can you bring her out?"

"No problem," said Stan, and in a second, in a way Duncan didn't really follow, picked the girl up and carried her through to the front room. The man who had fetched the stretcher stepped aside to let him by, and squinted at Duncan. "You the boyfriend?"

"No!"

The man, obviously not believing him, said, "Huh!" and followed his colleague through into the other room. Duncan went after him. The girl was on the stretcher, and Stan was spreading a red blanket over her. Seeing Duncan, Stan asked, "You coming?"

Duncan looked over his shoulder, towards the other room where Mrs Beckerdyke was slumped in her armchair.

"Her's all right," said the ambulanceman. "Bit dozy, but all right. You been having a right old time, eh? But no business of mine."

Duncan still wasn't sure what to do. He wanted to go with the girl and make sure she was all right, but the girl was being looked after, and maybe he should stay with the woman? What would Jesus have done?

He'd have stayed with the one who needed Him most… But He would have had the advantage of knowing which one that was.

The stretcher was outside now, clattering into the tiny front yard. The ambulance, big and white, was parked in the middle of the street, completely blocking it. "Make up your mind," Stan said, as he and the other man steered the stretcher though the gate. "We ain't got all day."

"I'll come." After all, the ambulancemen didn't seem concerned for Mrs Beckerdyke, and the woman did call herself a witch. The girl could still be saved.

He banged shut the door of number fifteen, Saint Etheldreda Street.

7

NOT ALONE IN THE HOUSE

Elizabeth Beckerdyke was woken by one of her own snores. She started up and, as she shifted from sleep to wakefulness, felt fear, like a slap round the face.

She had been sleeping in her armchair, which in itself was strange. Still more odd, a duvet was heaped over her, and she couldn't remember fetching it. Someone else must be in her house. Was that why her heart was skipping?

Dusk was thickening into dark, and the room waved before her eyes, meltingly becoming other dark, remembered places, where she didn't want to be. But she must be in one of them, because she was afraid, and there had to be a reason for the fear.

The room settled into familiarity as she became more awake. The big chimney-breast and the gas-fire that gave hardly any heat. The three doors, one to the stairs, one to the kitchen, and one into the front room. The ridiculous little mock chandelier, made from plastic, hanging from the centre of the ceiling; and the ugly wallpaper that she'd never liked, but had never bothered to change. It was Birmingham, surely, the little house in Saint Etheldreda Street that she rented because it was so cheap… But even while she recognized it, the very lines and blocks that made up the room seemed to change subtly, shifting their angles, tilting, slanting – oh, very subtly – so she couldn't be sure it was the same room. Had there been three doors before? Had the windows been so small? Had the alcoves beside the chimney-breast been quite so deep, holding such shadows?

The duvet fell in a heap to the floor as she hauled herself from the chair. Treading over it, she put on the nearest light – the clip-on lamp she had clipped to the curtain-rail near her computer-corner. A dull yellow light angled on to the ceiling and bounced from it over the rest of the room. The deep shadows, banished from the nearest alcove, crowded even more darkly into the further one. She was conscious, as she had never been before, of the room's three doors, and how her back must always be turned to at least one of them… It had to be her imagination, but whichever one was behind her seemed always to be stealthily opening to let something slide into the room – only to shut instantly the moment she looked at it.

There was someone else in the house, she knew it. She sensed something being carried to her on the very air – the warmth of someone else's body, perhaps, or the tiny sounds of cloth rubbing as someone moved, or of their breathing in a distant room. It stirred her hair.

Of course, the girl... Memory seeped back into her mind, in pictures and sounds, not words. She saw again the world of the dead and felt the exhilaration of flying there. She saw the frightened faces of the girl and the Scots boy – the Scots boy? Where had he –?

The scene outside her door came back to her. There had been a Scots boy fighting with that girl, and she had invited him in...

They were still in her house, then, this Scots boy and the girl. Inside her house, inside her, hiding from her. She looked round for a weapon, but there was nothing to hand that was either heavy or sharp enough.

She pulled open the door into the kitchen and, reaching in, snapped on the light. As she looked into the cramped and cluttered little space, her back crawled with her awareness of the room behind her and the other doors – were they opening?

There was no one in the kitchen, so she went in, letting the door swing shut behind her, guarding her back for at least a few seconds. The drainer beside the sink was full of crockery and cutlery, and she took from it a sharp, but slender knife before opening the door into the further passage.

The light from the kitchen fell on another of her knives lying on the passage floor, a large, cleaver-like knife with a strong triangular blade. Quickly, she stooped and picked it up, feeling a little safer and stronger with it in her hand. She pulled open the door of the bathroom, and looked into darkness, from which the white bath, basin and toilet bowl emerged, a vague grey. A whisper brushed her ear: the faintest of sniggers.

The pull for the light was several steps inside the door and she lunged for it and yanked it. The hard white lines of the bath and basin, the red floor, leaped into the light. No one was in the room; there was no one to snigger.

Leaving the light on, and holding the knife tightly, Elizabeth made her way back down the passage and through the kitchen into the living room. As she entered, she had the impression that the doors on the far side – the doors into the front room and to the stairs – were just closing after something had passed through them.

Her heart beat faster, and besides fear she felt an exhilaration, an eagerness to meet whoever was hiding in her house, and go for them, hurt them, drive them off. She slapped the broad, flat blade of the knife on her palm. She wasn't old and helpless yet. No one was going to intimidate her in her own home.

Crossing the little room, she opened the door that led through into the front room, turning sideways as she did so, to glance across at the kitchen door and not have to turn her back on it completely.

The front room was in darkness, except for the square of faint light where the streetlamps shone through the drawn curtains. Fleetingly, a shape was silhouetted against the window's square: a man's head and shoulders. In a blink, it was gone.

The light switch was on the other side of the room, by the front door – handy for when you came in from the street, but infuriatingly out of reach now. Elizabeth lunged across the room, her steps thumping heavily on the floor, her breathing loud with fright and hurry. Nothing, no one barred her way. She reached the light, snapped it on – and turned her knife on a pile of washing in an armchair, on an ironing board leaning against the mantelpiece... Calming a little, she looked more carefully about the room, and saw that she was alone. If someone had been standing in front of the window, they were gone now. Or she had imagined it.

She drew a deep, steadying breath and, leaving the light on, turned back towards her living room. She had only to search the upper floor now. As her back turned fully on the room she heard, just by her right ear, and not very loud but louder than a snigger, the soft "Ha, ha, ha," of laughter.

She stood still, lifting her head. "Now I know you," she said, aloud. This wasn't the girl. It was a man's laughter, but it wasn't the Scottish boy. All her memory came back. She knew what it was.

She had made a grave mistake.

All because she had wanted to prove herself more powerful than the crystal-wranglers and the candle-lighters. All because she had wanted to impress that little nothing, that ignorant, stupid little girl. And the Scots boy. Duncan. She had wanted to show him that she knew more, understood more, than could be found within the framework of his simplistic Christianity.

And so she did, but what did it matter? How could she boast of understanding when she was still driven by such petty vanity?

Because of petty vanity she had brought back – not only into this world, but into her very home – an unknown spirit. Not the stupid, lost, harmless little wraith of Zoe's sorry inamorato – which might squeak and gibber in dark corners, but could be dismissed easily enough – but a spirit of a very different kind. One that had deliberately sought her out, and disguised itself, in its determination to enter her world – and one which could only be supposed to be malign.

And she, knowing it to be malign, had guided it here.

She had bound it to her, in her blood, and had imagined she could control it – a woman holding a tiger on a leash and pretending it was a toy poodle.

But she could have controlled it. She could have paraded it before her little audience, and made it do tricks, and dismissed it again back to the other world – if only her audience had been content to watch and applaud. But the Scots boy...

Standing in the middle of her room, she clasped her hands together and rested them against her lips. While she had still been trancing, still bringing the spirit through, the Scots boy had stepped forward, and...

Oh, if only he knew it, he was a powerful witch, that boy. He could put Dorothy Bailey and all her cohorts to shame, and he'd probably never thought of energizing a crystal in his entire life.

He had thrown the spirit into panic and turmoil, and its writhings had thrown her back with it, into the other world. The bond she had made with it had snapped, and she had been lost and stunned...

Her Cat had found her, and she had gathered

herself together, and found her way back through dreams ... but while she had been wandering, a way had been left open, and that spirit, that malign spirit ... had found its way back here. It was loose.

The living room seemed smaller, the light so dim and yellow that it shadowed rather than illuminated. Walking firmly, still holding the knife tightly, she made for the door in the corner, the door to the stairs.

The switch for the light that lit the stairs was in the living room. She snapped it on before she opened the door.

The stairs were narrow, just wide enough for one person, and steep. Looking up, she could see nothing but the shabby carpet, and the pale wallpaper, torn in places and marked by a greasy trail where hands had dragged along it. On the landing above a naked light-bulb hung.

She held her hands before her face and stared until she glimpsed the faint, blurred halo around them. Frowning, concentrating, she made it swell, grow brighter and more violet. But she was tired. She could feel the effort dragging on her.

She climbed the stairs. Halfway up, the light went out, and again she heard – or thought she heard – the short, soft burst of laughter. The door at the bottom of the stairs was still open, and light came through it and lit the edges of the steps, though the light grew fainter as the steps went higher. The landing above was in darkness. But there was another light switch up there. She gripped the handle of her knife and went on climbing.

It became colder as she neared the landing, shockingly cold, like the dash of icy water on an icy night that makes the flesh clench and the heart stutter. She gasped, and clutched at the stair-rail. The air was thicker and heavier, harder to climb against – but she knew there was no running away from this enemy. She had no choice but to fight it and defeat it if she could. Gaining the landing, with effort, she snapped on the light.

It showed her the bare, ugly length of her landing, with the closed doors at either end – the further door seemed to be just shutting. She said, "I know what you are. I am on guard against you. In my body's hand I hold a knife; in my spirit's hand I hold a knife. I am not afraid of you."

There was no answer, not even a laugh. The light stayed on.

To her left, as she stood at the top of the stairs, was a bedroom door, closed.

She shoved it open, reached in and turned on the light. Holding the knife before her, she went in.

The room was cold with a deep chill that seemed to coat her skin – but it was always a cold room. It held nothing but an iron bedstead without a mattress, and several large boxes that she'd used to move house. Some were still not unpacked.

She opened the door to return to the landing, which was lit only by the light falling over her shoulder from the bedroom – and that vanished as the bedroom light went out. She stood in cold darkness.

Her hand found the landing light switch and snapped it on. A face was grinning into hers, so close it almost touched her. Light gleamed on the teeth and in the eyes. The face laughed, a soft, huffing sound. Before the sound ended, the face had gone, and there was nothing in front of her except the landing.

Her heart racketed, and her breath came in unsteady snatches. She swallowed hard. Though it had vanished almost as soon as she'd seen it, she knew the face. It had been the ghost's face, Gary's face. "I know you," she said. "I'm ready for you. I am not afraid."

A snigger: so faint that it might have been her own breathing, or her hair brushing on her collar.

She walked the length of the landing. The air was cold, she shivered. At the end of the landing were two doors, one directly in front of her, the other, the door of her bedroom, to her right.

She shoved open the door in front of her, reached her hand round the frame and switched on the light. The room was tiny and square, and as

127

cold as a freezer. It held an old sideboard, which had been there when she rented the house, and some rolls of wallpaper lying on the bare, grey floorboards.

So now there was only her bedroom. She pushed open the door. The light was already on, as if in welcome, and so was the gas-fire on the wall opposite the door. She could see its flames flickering. But the room was cold, not warm. She knew it was in there, waiting for her. She stepped through the door.

It was sitting on the bed, on top of the crumpled sheet. It looked like a young man, like Gary, who was dead. It turned its grinning face towards her and held out its arms, its hands gesturing her to come to it.

She stood in the centre of the room, holding the knife. "In the name of –"

Grinning, it said, "Come and have a cuddle."

"In the name of Woden, take off that shape. Look like what you are. In the name of Woden, and Freyr. And Christ. Leave me, and leave this place."

It rose from the bed, and its bones rattled as it moved, and rattled again as it came towards her.

"Don't pretend to be dead!" she cried. "In Woden's name, take on your real shape!"

It laughed, its mouth dropping open so far that it seemed its jaw would fall off, as a skull's jaw falls off. It lifted its arms to reach for her, its bones rattling, like dry sticks rattling together. Behind it she glimpsed, not the walls of her little bedroom, but some other place, indistinct, dark – it might have been broken walls she saw, or trees; and a dull red light, like a sunset or furnace fires. Not the world of Saint Etheldreda Street, then... The worlds had slipped and changed around her. She was going to have to fight.

A knife was still in her hand and with it she slashed at the long arms as they came at her; slashed and opened the flesh.

The thing recoiled from the knife, and dropped to the ground, twisting and folding on itself, no longer a man's shape. But it wasn't dismayed: it laughed. She peered down into the uncertain darkness around her feet, where something humped and crawled, trying to see what was there. "I have a torch, I have a torch in my hand!" she cried. It was hard to concentrate, with the air so thick, so hot and stinking and difficult to breathe, hard to make the torch rounded and real and bright – but it appeared in her hand. She felt its solidity, and its heat. Light poured from it, shining at her feet.

At her feet she saw a squirming thing, thick-bodied, like a great, muscular snake – but many-bodied too, like a nest of huge, thick, muscled, glistening worms – and rearing out of it a reddening, swollen face that was something like a man's, its expression an intent, single-minded malice.

In revulsion she quailed and stepped back – and the coils surged after her, slithering and looping to catch her legs. A mistake, to have shown fear. She went forward again, stooping, stabbing, trying to drive the knife into coils that twisted and slipped away from her. The malevolent head reared up, aiming for her – and in that instant she threw herself forward and down, tumbling over the slithering coils. She scowled as she made, in her mind, the image of what she needed to be and, as she went down, she changed, became a cat, large, muscled, clawed. Twisting round, she bit at the coils with longer, sharper teeth than a woman had, driving them in with more powerful jaws. She sank in her claws.

A thud on her spine that jarred her every bone came from the lashing of the heavy coils. Her mouth was filled with a vile taste from the slime that covered the thing. Twisting, she brought up her clawed hind paws to rake the thing, to dis-embowel it with all the power of her hind legs – and even as she did so, she felt her strength leaving her. She had travelled too far, travailled too much – just when she needed to reach for more strength, there was no more strength left.

The coils, winding about her, changed, became bulkier, furred – a snarling toothy face with blazing lantern eyes glared into hers. The thing had become a bigger cat, a tiger, and already she felt the pain of its claws. She needed to change again, quickly, and tried to find the space to think, to concentrate – but, in weariness, in panic, she slipped into the easiest change of all, and took on her own shape again.

The thing was quicker, far, far quicker, and before she could breathe or blink, it was a nest of worms, writhing, coiling. Something pushed between her legs, something muscled and powerful. Something slithered up her back. A jolt, driving against her, into her, pushing the air out of her in a groan – and as her mouth opened, something slithered against it, shoved over her tongue. She tried to close her teeth, but they met a substance like hard rubber that she could not bite – and then her throat was forced open by a probing, living thing that wriggled down into her, and she could not scream or protest.

She was taken.

8

HOSPITAL VISITS

Six beds were placed along each side of the ward: narrow beds with metal frames. The bedclothes were old, limp and worn with washing.

Beside each bed was a small, cheap white cupboard, square and graceless, cluttered with magazines and medicines. Curtains hung at each bed like shower curtains in flimsy nylon folds.

It was night, and the ward was in darkness except for the shaded lamp at the nurses' station. The dim yellow light took all colour even from those areas it lit, turning everything grey, or dark brown, or the yellow of nicotine-stained fingers, giving an impression of grubbiness and neglect.

Zoe lay one bed away from the nurse's station, because she'd tried to kill herself, and therefore needed watching. The bed next to her had been screened by the limp curtains, so that Zoe couldn't see the old woman who lay in it. She could hear her, though, wheezing, gasping, snoring, rattling.

"Is her dying?" Zoe had asked the nurse, some unmeasurable time ago, when she'd been helping Zoe into bed.

"She's fine," the nurse had said. "You mind your own business."

Zoe felt bruised, exhausted and weak, but still couldn't sleep, despite the fact that she suspected they'd given her something to dull her down and make her quiet. She drowsed and woke when the rattling and snoring from the next bed was too loud, and then she looked into the shadows around her, heard the sounds of breathing and creaking from the other beds, footsteps in the corridor, a soft laugh and a shuffling of papers from the nurses' office.

She thought: Still here. I've still got to wake up tomorrow, and the day after, and the day after that, and after that and after that, and get through all those days; and for why? So I can wake up the day after...

She thought: Pills are no good.

The old lady in the next bed choked and gurgled, and Zoe thought: Wish I could be her. Wish it was my time.

A train, she thought. Jump under it. That would be quicker, more certain. A block of flats. Climb over the balcony and just drop. Once you let go, if you could make yourself let go, there'd be no turning back, there'd be no chance of bloody nosy interfering types stopping her.

Being brought to hospital had been hell. She'd kept telling the ambulancemen that she wanted them to let her out, that she didn't want to be saved, that she wanted that Scots sod thrown out of the ambulance. They just kept shushing her and telling her that everything would be all right, – but it wasn't. The further the ambulance went, the sicker she felt, really horribly sick.

She thought it was the ambulance that was making her sick and asked them to stop. "No love, that's the pills," the ambulanceman said. "You throw up if you need to. We'll be at the hospital soon."

She tried to tell him again that she didn't want to go to any hospital, but the nausea welled up in her as soon as she tried to speak, so she couldn't. She had always hated being sick: the convulsions of stomach and throat, the smell, the mess. She'd lain quiet, trying to keep the vomit down, waiting for the endless journey to stop. It had to stop sooner or later, and then she could get out and walk away.

But she'd felt increasingly strange. Her eyes

were hard to keep open; she felt herself sinking into sleep – and then a heave from her stomach would wake her, and she'd see the whiteness of the ambulance and the strange man's face, and think: Where is this? What's going on? She couldn't remember what time of day it was, or what day, and it was a struggle to sort anything out in her head.

When the ambulance finally had stopped, they'd lifted her out on the stretcher and carried her into the hospital, and she hadn't felt well enough to make even a squeak about it. She just wanted to lie still, and not have to think, and try not to be sick. Walking away anywhere just hadn't been possible. She felt so strange in her head that she didn't think she would be able to sit up, let alone stand up.

She felt so ill, she thought she must be dying anyway and then a lively little panic leaped up inside her, and she would have begged them to save her life if she'd been well enough to talk. Then a sudden calm would come over her, and she'd think that the sooner she died, the better. There'd be nothing more to worry about then. But as soon as she thought that, her bowels were gripped by the icy terror of near death – real death, not fantasy death. It was confusing. She didn't want what she thought she'd wanted. She wasn't who she'd thought she was. Except that she did, and was.

Doctors and nurses were supposed to be kind, but they weren't. "Well, you're a silly little madam, aren't you?" a woman said to her, slamming down the metal side of her bed. Zoe didn't know if she was a doctor or a nurse or a cook – she was just an angry someone in a white coat. "Don't you think I've got better things to do than pander to you, you silly, *silly* girl?" the woman said.

Zoe leaned over the side of the bed and threw up on the floor. Her hands got in the way, and the puke felt scalding hot as it fell on them. Her gullet felt as if it was turning inside out, and would come out of her throat along with the vomit, which spattered over the angry woman's legs and shoes and on to the tiled floor.

The woman had sighed, loudly, and yelled for a nurse. "At least that saves me giving you something to make you sick," she said. "Now, listen to me, how many tablets did you take?"

Zoe held up her hands, from which vomit dripped. She had sick all round her mouth and chin. Having told everyone that she wanted to die, she wouldn't change her tune now. "Leave me alone."

"Oh, for God's sake, spare me the soap opera!" the woman yelled, really furious, making Zoe draw back and blink in surprise. The woman stooped close to her, glaring. "I'm busy, do you understand? I'm busy. So stop mucking me about.

136

Don't you know how dangerous paracetamol is, you idiot girl? Don't you know what it will do to your liver? It'll turn it into dead meat, that's what, unless we get the antidote inside you in time. Now, how many did you take and how long ago?"

Zoe had been feeling very odd – flimsy, transparent – and this loud, angry woman, shoving her face and glaring eyes close up, so big and so very solid ... Zoe didn't feel able to cope with her. If she answered, and was good, the woman might go away. And, if she allowed herself to be overwhelmed, and answer, they might save her, without her having to ask them to save her. In her mind she could see the bottom of the paracetamol drum and the tablets clustered together. "Only about ten or so."

"Now we're getting somewhere. And how long ago?"

It was beyond Zoe to work it out. It seemed a long, long time ago, far away in some cotton-woolly distant time.

"Never mind," said the woman. "Just you behave now and do what the nurses tell you, or I shall really lose my temper. I'm sick and tired, *sick and tired*, of dealing with bloody thoughtless people like you, who down a packet of paracetamol to make their boyfriend feel bad, and then come along here when they start feeling ill, and I have to tell them they've buggered up their liver and they're going to die. They're going to die, and they've changed their minds and beg me to save them, and there's *nothing* I can do. Nothing. You think I enjoy that? Do you? Do you?"

"No," Zoe said meekly, since it was what the woman seemed to want her to say.

The woman went away after that, and the nurses came, and made her drink things, and put drips in her arms, and bandaged her wrist. Zoe felt so distant and awful, she let them get on with it, until they started asking her if there was anyone they could phone for her.

"Leave me alone."

"What about your mum and dad, love? Let them know where you are, that you're all right? Your boyfriend? A friend, eh?"

The last thing Zoe wanted was people fussing round, telling her things "for her own good" and asking what she'd gone and done something like this for. "Go away."

"C'mon love, tell us your name, or a phone number."

"Leave me alone, just leave me alone."

They sighed, and left her alone while they wheeled her into a lift and took her up to the ward. "Am I going to die?" she asked the nurse who helped her into bed.

"No, you're not going to die. You've been a very silly girl, though. If you go playing silly games like this again, you might not be so lucky the next time."

Zoe was left to lie in the bed and look at the nylon curtains drawn round the bed next to her. Still here, she thought. Still not with Gary. It was harder to get out of this world than it seemed.

Her gullet and chest and belly ached from vomiting. She felt weak and wretched and couldn't be bothered to do anything except lie still. Even when the Scots boy came to her bed, and sat on a plastic chair beside it, she couldn't find the strength to swear at him, or tell him to go away. She just turned her head away from him and lay still and, after a while, he went away by himself.

Good riddance, she thought to herself. I hope I never see you again.

"I don't know her name," Duncan said. "Sorry, can't help you."

"Well, wait in the waiting area, please, sir. You'll be much better in the waiting area. There's nothing you can do, you'll only be in the way. Please, sir, wait in the waiting area. Someone will come and tell you how she is in a few minutes."

Duncan had gone back to the waiting area, a place painted in two tones of grey, with dim little alcoves and low ceilings, architect-designed to oppress and depress. The scuffed and torn grey benches around the walls of the alcoves were

139

almost all empty, and the few people waiting sat well apart, without looking at each other or speaking.

Duncan took a seat as far from everyone else as he could, and waited. There was nothing to look at except the grey tiles on the floor and the grey walls. Nothing to read – but before he could get bored a woman with a clipboard came looking for him. "Excuse me, were you with the overdose who's just been brought in?"

"A girl?" Duncan said. "Took paracetamol?"

"Only we need to know her name and address." The woman looked expectantly at him, her pen ready in her hand.

"I told the others. I don't know her name or address." The woman looked at him disbelievingly. "I don't," he said.

"But she's got no identification on her at all. No credit cards, no memberships, no address book – nothing at all but a purse with a bit of money in it."

Duncan stared wonderingly at the woman as she stared at him. She found it surprising that the girl had so little on her. He shrugged. "I've got none of those things either." He didn't even have a purse, or a wallet. He carried his money loose in his pockets.

"We can't contact her next of kin without having some kind of ID," said the woman.

Duncan shrugged again. "Can't help you. Sorry."

The woman's brows flicked up and her mouth pursed, in a way that made clear her opinion of him and the girl. "Sorry to have bothered you," she said, and went away.

Duncan sat down again, and waited some more. He became hungry. After an hour, when no one had called him, or come to find him, he went to reception. "Can you tell me how my friend is? She was brought in. Overdose."

"What's her name?" the receptionist asked.

"Sorry. I don't know."

The receptionist gave him a what-do-you-expect-me-to-do-then? look.

"She was about my age," Duncan said. "Bit younger, maybe. Blonde hair. Fastened up on top." He gestured vaguely, trying to describe how the girl did her hair.

"Give me a minute," the receptionist said. "I'll see what I can do."

Duncan leaned on the desk and waited for another long time before the receptionist came back. "Your friend's out of the woods. She's been taken up to Ward C4, just for the night. She can go home tomorrow."

"Could I see her?" The receptionist told him how to find the ward, and said he'd have to have a word with the nurse on duty. He went outside into a chill wind, and across a grey yard, following signs directing him to Block C. A grey, metal-framed door in a brick wall admitted him to dim, narrow corridors and claustrophobic staircases. He glanced into wards where people sat looking bored and sad, and finally he found Ward C4. There was a nurse there, a young one. When he explained that he was looking for the girl who'd taken an overdose, she said, "Oh, you mean our Zoe."

"Zoe?" Duncan said. He liked the name.

"That's her name; she told me. You can look in on her so long as you're quick, you're quiet, and you don't disturb anybody else."

Zoe was in bed and he thought, at first, she was asleep. She looked pale and sick: her lovely olive skin had gone a sort of greyish-yellow, and her dyed blonde hair made her even more pallid. Her face, instead of being pretty and lively, now looked slack and plain. Pitiful.

When he moved the plastic chair closer to the bed and sat on it, she stirred, opened her dark eyes – blood-shot now – and looked at him. He smiled, and was about to say hello, when she closed her eyes again and turned her face away. She did it pointedly. Duncan closed his mouth on his unspoken greeting and, after a moment, got up and left.

As he walked out of the hospital grounds he

wasn't sure what to do, but his belly, pinching and complaining, decided that for him. Get something to eat. It took him an hour to walk back into the city proper, walking alongside busy, noisy roads, and by the time he got there, he was hungrier than ever.

He knew a church where they ran a cheap canteen in the basement. It wasn't his church, which didn't have a building of its own. This was a Baptist church, or Methodist – something like that – but it was OK. The people were all right. They gave him a big bowl of thick soup, a big bread roll and a cup of coffee for a pound, and the old woman who served him, who knew him, wrapped a thick slice of home-made fruit cake in a paper napkin and dropped it into his pocket, together with a chocolate biscuit. "You get yourself outside of that," she said. "And sit and have a warm."

While eating, Duncan wondered what he should do now. Go back to the hostel and forget the girl and the woman, he thought. Why not? Neither wanted anything to do with him. He'd done all he could for them.

Somebody, though, should check up on the woman. Make sure that she was all right.

Yeah, but why him?

Why not him? And who else would do it?

He could phone the police, get them to go round.

That was dodging things, though. What would Jesus do? And once he asked himself that, there was only one answer.

After he'd eaten, he walked over to Saint Etheldreda Street, and past the cars and through the litter to the door of number fifteen. He stood in the little paved yard for a long time, wanting to knock, but not raising his hand. Partly, he was embarrassed. If the woman came to the door, he didn't know what he could say. She might be angry. She might not remember him. It would be awkward.

But there was more than embarrassment. It took him a while to realize that he was afraid. The door in front of him was ordinary: a large glass panel in a thin white frame, with a letterbox at the bottom. But he was afraid of it. Of what was behind it.

He reminded himself of the woman inside, whom he'd last seen slumped unconscious in her armchair. The ambulancemen had said she would be all right; probably she was all right, but someone had to make sure. *He* had to make sure.

He stepped closer to the door and put his ear to it. From inside he could hear nothing: no television, no radio, no sound of anyone moving about. And then he stepped sharply back, almost to the gate.

It wasn't anything he'd heard. Or not, anyway, anything he'd heard with his ears. If the blood can be said to hear, then he heard it with his blood. There was *something* in the house.

Well, of course there was. The woman.

Something else. Something that knew he was standing outside the door. What he had sensed was *it* sensing him.

Once before he had been close to this thing, when he had moved between the girl, Zoe, and the ghost. That feeling swept through him again, of being a wavering, guttering flame, almost snuffed into darkness. He started to shake, his muscles jumping and quivering on his bones, and he backed out of the gate on to the pavement, and then, quickly, away down the street.

At the end of the street, he was able to stop. He ought to go back, he knew that he should, but he didn't move from where he stood.

Jesus would have gone back. Jesus would have tried to help the woman. Found out if she was hurt, or even alive.

But this time, he couldn't persuade himself. He couldn't make himself do what he ought to do. He was too much afraid.

He crossed the street to get even further from number fifteen, and stood in front of the big pub. What to do now?

He could go back to his room in the hostel, where he would sit and brood all evening over what he should have done and had failed to do.

He could try to sleep and lie awake all night. He could go out to the pub, to try and find distraction, and be the sober man among the drunks…

He went back to the hospital. The girl was there on her own, unwell, and none of her family knew where she was. Somebody ought to be with her. And it made him feel better, after running away from number fifteen, to do something that he knew he should.

He was tired by the time he got back to the hospital, and cold. The place was dark, and largely deserted. Without bothering to go to reception, he walked through yards to C Block and made his way up to Ward C4. No one was about. No one stopped him.

At the door to the ward, he stopped. He couldn't see a nurse anywhere. So he went in.

The big windows shone glassily in the darkness, black except where they reflected back the dim yellow lights of the ward. One woman, at the far end of the ward, was sitting up in bed, reading, and looked at him a moment, without curiosity. Others shifted in their beds at his footsteps.

He came to Zoe's bed. She was lying quietly on her side, perhaps sleeping. The plastic chair was still beside the bed, and he sat on it again. It occurred to him that, whether Zoe woke or not, this was a good place for him to stay for the night. Quiet. Warm. Out of the rain. He got up and pulled the curtain partly round the bed – not far, but enough to screen him from anyone looking along the ward, just in case he shouldn't be there. Then he sat down again.

The ward fell asleep. The woman further down the ward turned off her lamp and lay down. It was impossible for Duncan, sitting upright in a chair, to fall asleep, but with his arms folded across his chest he fell into a sleepy trance. Thoughts buzzed dozily, lazily about his head, repeating themselves and repeating themselves like a looped tape – he wasn't listening to them anyway. Hazily, he saw pictures in his mind: impressions of colours: green, violet, a doorway, a cat, green circles… It meant something, but he didn't know what and it didn't matter.

He woke when someone came round the edge of the curtain he'd partly drawn. He sat up abruptly in his chair, thinking it was the nurse.

The woman stood by the side of the bed, looking down at Zoe. It wasn't the nurse. It was the witch. Mrs Beckerdyke.

Duncan sat up straighter, pushing himself against the back of the chair. The sight of the woman, the dark block of her in the dim light, sent a shock of alarm through him, set his heart beating faster and made his breathing falter. It was the same senseless fear he had felt a few hours earlier, outside her door. He didn't know the reason, but his body did.

The woman looked down at the girl in the bed and said, "Zoe?" Then she lifted her head and looked across the bed, straight at Duncan. Her face was partly shadowed but, even so, at the sight of it, he started up from his chair, ready to fight or run.

It was the face of the witch, but it was as if the woman's features had been smoothed on to an egg. The eyes stared at him, fiercely focused, sharply on him, but the rest of the face was unlined and bland. The heavy lines around the mouth had gone, as had the crinkles under the eyes – but also the hollow below the lower lip. The face didn't look younger or more beautiful – the hollows under the brows were smoother, less deep; the nose was more flattened, becoming lost in the face. It was unmistakably Mrs Beckerdyke – it was also not a face.

"Hello Duncan," said the witch, and smiled.

He took a step away from the bed, and looked round, looking for help, or for somewhere to run. When she smiled, her face didn't change. The mouth moved, spread sidelong, but her cheeks didn't crease, her eyes didn't change shape.

Zoe stirred in the bed, and the witch looked down at her again. "Zoe. Wake up. I'm here to see you."

Zoe moved, rolling on to her back. She brought her arms up beside her head, stretching. "Oh." She sat up. "You."

Duncan stood frozen, a couple of steps from the bed. He looked from the girl to … the woman? Zoe looked at the woman without any reaction. She didn't seem to notice anything unusual.

Is it me? Duncan thought. Am I dreaming?

"Gary is waiting for you," said Mrs Beckerdyke. As she spoke, Duncan breathed in a rank, strong stink that drifted towards him – a breath-catching stink of old sweat and shit – and in the same moment, he felt the skin shrink on his arms in a sudden chill, as if he had touched against ice. He drew back another step.

"Gary?" Zoe said. She was still looking up at the woman, without shrinking back from the cold and the stink.

"I've brought him back to you," Beckerdyke said. "As I said I would."

"For a second," Zoe said. "He went again as soon as he come. That's no good."

"But I can do better, Zoe. I can bring him again – or we can take you to where he is."

Zoe looked up, taken by the idea.

"You must come back to us, Zoe. You must come soon."

"Us", the witch said. For no reason he could understand, this single little word made Duncan's heart leap with fright, and his breath stopped. And, aware of his fright, the egg-smooth face lifted again, and the fierce eyes sharpened on him.

They seemed to fix on him with force: he felt a jolt, as if from a blow, and wanted to run away, but the stare held him in place. "You must both come," the woman said, and the stench thickened, as if it was her breath. "We can talk, Duncan. About Gods and things." She smiled again, that unsmiling smile.

Zoe looked round and saw Duncan for the first time. "Not him! It was his fault. It was him – interfering! He was why Gary went."

"He can help us bring Gary back. You must both come. We want both of you. Come."

The woman turned and walked away. Duncan watched her with such care – the way she moved, the way her long skirt shifted with her, the way loose tendrils of her hair bobbed. It was all so real, so natural, just like a woman walking. He felt his muscles tightening, becoming more and more tense as he watched and waited for the moment when the thing would give up the pretence and simply vanish ... but it dwindled into the dimness of the corridor and the obscurity of notices stuck over the glass windows, and he could not be sure whether it had vanished or simply moved out of sight.

He remained standing where he was, searching his mind for some idea of what he should do, of where he could find help, of who he should ask... After a few moments he realized that he was shaking again, and that he felt sick. Of one thing he was sure: that neither he nor Zoe should ever go near number fifteen, Saint Etheldreda Street.

Zoe was getting out of the bed.

"What you doing?" he said.

She glanced at him, and her expression became hostile and sneering. Without answering him, she turned away and pulled clothes out of the locker beside her bed. She began to put them on.

"Have they said you can go?" he asked, going nearer to her.

"Piss off."

"You should stay here until they say you can go."

"Nobody tells me what to do," she said. "Not them, not you. So piss off and leave me alone."

"Where are you going?"

"Away from here and away from you."

"Don't go back there," he said. "Zoe. Don't."

She finished pulling on her clothes. Her shirt was stained with sick: he could smell it. Glaring at him, she said, "How d'you know my name?"

"Don't go back there. Whatever you do, don't go to that place."

She looked at him with distaste, her mouth pulling into a grimace. "Listen," she said. "Why don't you just piss off back to Scotland where you come from, and – drop dead and rot."

Then she turned and walked out of the ward – walking just where that thing had walked, as if it had marked out a path for her.

He followed her out into the corridor. As she headed towards the stairs, a nurse bobbed out of a doorway and said, "Where are you going?"

Zoe ignored her, until the nurse stepped into her way. Then she said, "You can't make me stop."

"You should stay until doctor's seen you in the morning."

"Piss off. I'm not staying."

The nurse spread her arms to block Zoe's way as she tried to go past, but the nurse was looking at Duncan. "Who are you? How did you get in here?"

Duncan shrugged. "Walked in."

"You shouldn't be here —" The nurse turned abruptly to Zoe, who had shoved past her. "You really would be best advised to wait until the doctor's seen you."

"You can't tell me what to do, you can't make me stay here."

"Are you discharging yourself, then?" the nurse asked. "If you're going to insist on that, you'll have to sign a paper."

"I'm signing nothing," Zoe said, and swung off down the corridor.

Duncan skipped past the glaring nurse and, as Zoe started to run, ran after her. "Zoe, listen. Come back. Zoe, you mustn't – it's dangerous. Zoe!"

She kept going, and didn't even look at him.

9

GARY

The body of Elizabeth Beckerdyke sat, upright and stately, in her armchair. On her lap was her cat, in a muddle of matted fur, bones, meat and blood. She rammed her fingers under the fur, pushing it back, and grasped a leg, twisting to break the sinews and tear it off. The blood seeped under her nails, blackening them. Her hands were gloved in thickening blood. More blood was about her mouth, and she chewed hard on the tough, raw meat.

From somewhere inside Elizabeth Beckerdyke's head, Elizabeth Beckerdyke herself looked out through the eyes, catching a sidelong, twisted view. None of the lines or corners of the room seemed at the right angle, and none of the angles fitted together. The colours were all wrong: too pale, all fading to grey, or blurring into sepia rainbows.

Elizabeth took fright and struggled – struggled as one drowning in a dream struggles to wake, or as one caught in clinging mud struggles to evade it – but the dream, the mud, held her hard. Once she had shrugged off her body and flown into other worlds – but now she was too tightly enclosed. She hadn't the space to stretch and reach out. She was crowded close, pinned into a corner by the other thing that filled so much of her body's space.

Exhausted by the effort to escape, she fell quiet, and again peered out of her own eyes, gaining an oblique and slanted view, as if she peered through a narrow keyhole. She saw, emerging from the papered wall of the small house, a vast fish – it had legs and arms as well as fins. She watched it for as long as she could as it swam through the air of the room – but then it was out of her sight. Peering downwards, she saw bugs as big as rats crawling about the hearth, chittering faintly. Into her sight – drifting down from above, as if they came through the ceiling, she glimpsed legs, claws, tails. A whole creature, a strange thing, passed her slowly, sinking vertically. She strained to see, and saw it sink through the floor.

Craving some ordinary sight of her own world,

she turned her eyes towards the television, and saw the clock on the video. Its green numbers had become white against a black background, and the minutes streamed by continually, flickering, with less than a second's pause between them.

Her own fingers – or, the fingers that had been hers – raised a gobbet of meat to her mouth. She bridled, tried to draw back her head from it, tried to turn her head aside – but the strings that attached her consciousness to her body had been cut. She could no longer take her hand from her mouth or close her teeth, simply by thinking of the action. Now, another pulled her strings.

The meat went into her mouth filling it with warm, wet blood, with its sour, coppery taste. Her teeth clenched on it, against her will, chewing. She felt the satisfaction of that other: not the satisfaction of hunger, but of curiosity.

And then, as blood oozed between her teeth and went down her throat, she thought: I dare to do this.

I know what this is like. I understand. And knowledge is power.

Stick with us, kid, said the other – those others – who crowded her in her own skull. Stick with us, and you'll know what others don't dare to know. Stick with us and you'll have power that others are afraid to have.

Elizabeth bit down on the meat in her mouth,

adding her will to that of the Other in her head. Blood was life. In life was death. This was the way of a shaman – and it had nothing to do with pretty crystals and scented candles, nothing to do with wearing floaty dresses and snipping little sprigs in herb-gardens. A shaman's way was often cruel and ugly, and it took courage to follow. Those who weren't strong enough turned back in disgust and fright.

Elizabeth Beckerdyke would not turn back.

Little ones are coming, said the Other. They are running along to us now. We can wriggle into them, and out of them and into others –

As rot passes from one fruit to another and eats them all, Elizabeth thought, and she flinched from what she might be setting free…

Here come the little ones, said the Other. We can play with them. Make their flesh your bread, make their blood your drink. Eat their hearts for courage and their brains for knowledge, and know them through and through, as the little things don't dare to know.

Elizabeth flinched again. The power of Cold and Darkness must be acknowledged, but… But to flinch from them was weakness and cowardice. Elizabeth Beckerdyke would not turn back! Only the cruel and the strong could understand that without Death there could be no change, and no new beginnings.

We are legion, they said; and you are with us.

* * *

Zoe stumped along rapidly, her shoulders working, her fists and her jaw clenched. She would no longer speak to, or even look at Duncan.

He trailed after her, trudging just beside her or, sometimes, walking on the other side of the street. He no longer tried to persuade her, or spoke to her at all, though the fear of what they would find in Saint Etheldreda Street steadily grew in him.

He wondered if he should leave her and go in search of help. Go and knock at Petra's door and ask for help from other members of his church – perhaps call out the pastor. But while he was fetching them, what would happen to Zoe? He had no choice but to stay close by her. He prayed as they walked: "Jesus, protect us. Jesus, guard us. Jesus, watch over us…" He put such feeling into the prayer that he felt it going out of him and reaching away into the night. It would, he hoped, reach whatever power it was that he called "Jesus".

After walking by car after car after car, Zoe reached the gate of number fifteen, and Duncan, running a few paces, caught her up and grabbed her arm, pulling her up short. "No, you've *got to* listen. There's nothing good for you in there. Gary isn't in there, never was."

She grimaced and drove her elbow backwards into his chest. He let her go, and she pulled open the gate and darted inside, slamming it after her. He leaned against the gate and watched as she beat on the door's glass panel with her fist. "Don't. Don't, Zoe, don't."

She gave him a look of hatred over her shoulder, but didn't answer.

The door opened, and there stood the big woman, the witch, Elizabeth Beckerdyke. Except that Duncan, looking at her, didn't think it was Elizabeth Beckerdyke at all. Or, not only Elizabeth Beckerdyke.

She stood against the darkness of the doorway, the room dark behind her, and she was lit only by the light falling from the streetlamps. The broad rounds of her shoulders and breasts and hips were wrapped in dark wool that stirred gently, like the thickness of fur. And her face – it had that taut smoothness again; as if it had been wrapped around the smoothness of an egg. It was without lines, but not young. It was bland, yet held depths of malice. The very sight of the woman roused in Duncan the same unreasoning loathing as did the sight of a large black spider.

Without a word – but with a smile that didn't wrinkle her face – Beckerdyke stood aside and held open the door for Zoe to go in.

"Zoe – don't!" Duncan reached out his hand to stop her, but she walked past the witch and into the house without giving him a glance.

Still the witch stood in the doorway, waiting. She was looking, and smiling, at Duncan.

It was a challenge: Duncan knew that even as he started to shake. Zoe didn't know what she was entering into, as she walked through that door. But he did know. And the witch stood waiting for him to run away.

He opened the gate, crossed the little yard with a couple of strides, and passed through the doorway. His flesh shrank on his bones as he passed close by the witch. He felt the cold from her. Beneath his breath he said, "Jesus, be with me. Help me." He prayed not only with his mouth, but with his heart – he felt it ache with the urgency and need he felt.

Nothing answered him. There was none of the warmth and peace that Jesus had brought when He'd come before.

Zoe hurried through the dimly lit front room, past chairs piled high with washing, past stacked chairs and boxes. One step took her through the tiny hallway between the rooms, and she crashed into the back room, where the air was thick with heat, and stopped so suddenly she almost stumbled. Gary was sitting on the sofa, fully dressed this time, his elbows on his knees, his head in his hands, staring at the floor. He didn't look up. He didn't move at all.

A sweet, almost painful gladness filled Zoe.

Unable to speak, she stood staring, oblivious to everything except the fact that Gary was back again. Alive again. She wanted to hug him and feel his warmth and squeeze his solid body in her arms, but she was afraid to move in case, somehow, she made him vanish, as he'd vanished before. Look up, she thought, look up and see me. See me and come to me. Gary remained motionless.

Duncan came into the room a moment after her. At the sight of Gary a sickly, greasy cold crept over his skin, seeping in through his pores, sinking to his bones. The room stank, filling his nose and mouth until his throat spasmed and he retched. "Jesus," he said, and put a hand over his face. "Please, Jesus." Why wasn't Jesus coming? He felt panicky. He didn't know how he expected Jesus to come – maybe not in person, in a blaze of light. But he could feel the threat and danger, could smell it, could taste it in the air – and where was Jesus? Where was He?

Zoe was so calm. She just stood there, staring. She didn't seem to notice the stink, the cold... From behind his hand, he said, "Zoe. Come on." She didn't hear him. Duncan looked again at what held her attention so intently.

Gary hadn't moved, even slightly, during all the seconds they'd been in the room. If he looked at Gary's head, it was clear, sharp, in focus; and so was the collar about his neck. But the rest of his figure, the rest of his clothes, faded off into a coloured blur. There was a sense of it being there, but nothing was clear. Yet if he looked at, say, Gary's foot, then the trainer and the hem of the trousers were clear, even to the stitching and the lettering on the trainer – but now the upper part of the figure had blurred. It made him feel dizzy, unreal.

"Come on. Out the back and through the gardens." He grabbed at Zoe's arm, since she still didn't hear him. "That's us, come on."

Only at his touch did Zoe become aware that he was there, and then an immense irritation swept her. Bad enough that he should have followed her, worse that he thought he had a right to pull at her and order her about. Wrenching her arm free, she shoved him, sending him staggering back against the flimsy, gate-legged table behind him. He clutched at the table, fearing it was about to collapse. Magazines and letters slid off on to the floor as he tried to catch them.

Zoe, turning from him, saw that Gary was still seated on the sofa, still exactly as he had been, staring at the floor. The little commotion caused by her shoving the Scots boy hadn't made him disappear. She felt herself almost melting with delight. "Gary?"

Duncan, regaining his balance, saw from the corner of his eye that the witch-woman had entered the room, closing the door behind her.

Instantly, the whole of Gary snapped into focus. He looked up and smiled, and at that movement, Duncan felt his heart clench small. The air in the room had tightened, and was so thick with stink he could hardly draw it into his lungs. In his mind, or perhaps in his heart, he cried out: Jesus! Help! We need You! He felt the first pressure of a dreadful, hopeless fear: that there would be no answer and no help.

"Sweetheart!" Gary said, looking at Zoe. "Come here and give us a kiss!" The face was smiling, but it was as egg-smooth, as bland, as the witch's.

Zoe moved. She was going to that thing. Duncan knew that he was outmatched, that he could not hope to win here. But he had less than a second in which to act, and he could not just stand by. Lunging forward, he caught hold of Zoe and snatched her back.

Zoe, staggering backwards, yelled with anger. Stumbling, she caught her leg against the armchair behind her and, helpless to prevent herself, fell into the chair, dragging the Scots nutter down with her. He landed on top of her, his bony shoulder and hip punching into her. "Ow! You stupid! Stupid bugger!" She smacked her knuckles into him several times, meaning to hurt as much as she could, and she tried to shove him off her – but although he didn't look very big, she couldn't shift his dead weight.

Duncan let her punch and struggle – she hurt him, but his attention was on the thing, which had risen from the sofa and was coming towards them, its smooth egg-face malformed into a smile of sorts. "Jesus! Jesus!" He was realizing that Jesus wasn't going to help.

"Who's this character?" Gary said, and held out a hand towards him. "Here y'are mate. I'll give you a hand up."

Zoe stretched out her own hand, crying, "Gary, Gary!" – but this Scotsman had the nerve to knock her hand down, and used his weight to push her further back into the chair. "Get *off*!"

"Father, Son and Holy Ghost!" Duncan said. "Lord God, Our Father! Deliver us from Evil! Please! *Please!*"

A religious *nutter*, Zoe thought.

The thing that looked like Gary loomed over Duncan, reaching towards him. At its hand's approach, Duncan felt his skin creep as if hair had brushed across it – and then the thing swung round on its heel, hunching its shoulders and looking back over its shoulder. Its face had gone bland again.

It can't touch me, Duncan realized. It's afraid to touch me. A little hope leaped up inside him again.

"Little Christian," said Beckerdyke, from her corner by the door, and Duncan looked at her. Her face, too, was so smooth. Her eyes seemed to have moved further apart. There were no lines left in her face at all. "So proud of being a Christian. A brand new, shiny clean Christian. You, who slept for days in the same clothes, and puked down his clothes and wore them, and pissed himself and didn't know it, he was so drunk. Such a Christian!"

Duncan felt the shock as if he'd been punched over the heart. Everything she said was true. But how did she know? He had never told her. Paranoia woke in his brain. Who had told on him? And then a deeper fear, and a deeper cold. The thing didn't need to be told. "I believe," he said, "in Jesus Christ, the Son of God, Who –"

Zoe gathered her knees into her chest and bent her elbows against Duncan's back. With a heave, she managed to lever him out of the chair. He toppled to the carpet, landing on his hands and knees, saying, "– died on the Cross to save me, and –"

Beckerdyke laughed. "You. You set yourself up as a shining light for others. And all the time you're a shit-in-your-pants and puke-down-your-shirt little shit, drunk as a skunk, and nothing more... A meat-bag, full of pus and shit and piss, waiting to putrefy, that's all you are."

Every word was spoken with a still harsher bite, and Duncan felt that he was being cut away, piece by piece, made littler and littler until, indeed, he was no more than a lump of meat. On his hands and knees he clenched his fists, dragging his nails through the dusty carpet, hanging on to the knowledge that these things couldn't touch him. "I never hurt anybody but me! And that's done with!"

Beckerdyke laughed appreciatively, and he realized that he shouldn't have stepped back into self-defence. "Oh, the righteous pride of a walking, talking turd! How dare you come here, thinking yourself the equal of us. How dare you even lift your eyes to look at me."

Zoe, baffled, stopped listening to them. Let them rabbit; that was their thing. Gary was looking down at her and smiling. She scrambled to her feet.

Duncan, rising to his knees, had his back to Zoe, and didn't see what she did. "I don't set myself up..." No, he shouldn't speak of himself, he shouldn't attempt to defend himself. "I know, I know –"

"What do you know?" Beckerdyke asked. "You've been alive for less time than it takes me to blink my eye, and what do you know? How to piss and shit and puke yourself like a baby, that's all you know."

"That doesn't matter!" Duncan shouted; and he knew that it didn't. He knew that if he stood up to his neck in a pile of his own shit, *it didn't matter –*

but that this enemy would keep dragging his attention back to the shit, as if it was *all* that mattered.

Oh, why was he alone here? Where was *help*?

But he wasn't alone. Zoe. Whipping round, he saw her entering into the embrace of the thing that she thought was Gary. "No!" With both hands he grabbed at the nearer of Gary's arms and tried to pull it away from the girl. "No, I won't let you hurt her!"

He didn't know what happened. Something hit him in many places at once, lifted him up – it was like the impact of a heavy, speeding truck. His breath stopped, his head rang. Another impact stopped his onward rush: he hit the closed door to the kitchen with a thud that cracked the wooden panelling. Like a dropped doll, he fell to the floor. He couldn't move, and the world had stopped.

Zoe's mouth fell open. Gary had seized the Scots boy by the front of his jacket, had jerked him up off his feet and then had thrown him – just lifted and thrown him – across the room. She turned and stared at Gary. He was strong, she knew, but she'd never known that he was that strong.

Gary grinned, and joy rose up in her. He'd thrown the Scots boy aside for her. Because he was jealous. Because he loved her. He was really back with her. She really, really had him again. How or why she didn't care. "C'mere," Gary said and, thankfully, she went into his arms and felt their hardness close round her as her head fitted into the hollow of his shoulder. His hand stroked down the length of her back, and she felt his soft little touches on her head and cheek as he kissed her.

"Give us a kiss," he said.

She lifted up her face, and their mouths met – and through the tunnel of their mouths, his tongue came shoving, like a thick, slick, muscular snake. Down her throat the snake pulsed, and she swallowed and was swallowed.

10

A BATTLE

For Duncan, after he hit the kitchen door and thumped to the floor, everything was removed to a distance. What he saw was hazy, indistinct, ringed with a white glare. What he heard was muffled and unclear. Only the pain in his shoulder was close and fierce. But he heard Beckerdyke's voice, though it fluttered and boomed. "You won't let us? *You* won't let *us*? You pride-fallen bag of shit, you'll tell *us* what we may and may not do? We'll take you down."

Duncan gritted his teeth against passing out. He got his knees to the hard floor – his head spun and he hardly knew which way up he was, there was such pain in his shoulder, where he'd struck against the door… He sensed a bulk nearing him, a cold, a stronger stench.

He tried to stand, and a glaring whiteness pressed in on his vision and his head from either side… A dark hole opened in the whiteness, and he fell into it.

Down into the darkness, down, down deep – no longer falling, but swimming. He felt the effort of moving his arms and legs against the heavy water, he felt cold water flowing over his skin. Yet he drew breath, and his chest moved. *How am I breathing?* he thought. He was underwater and going deeper, but he breathed. Turning, he tried to swim for the surface – but where was the surface? There was no pull towards it and he had no idea, in the darkness, whether he was rising, or going deeper. Panic began.

Where had his enemies gone? They'd been around him, pressing closer – where were they hiding? He thrashed about in darkness, turning this way, now that, trying to spot them before they sprang on him. He saw nothing but darkness – were they hidden in the dark? It was desolating. Why was he alone? Where was help? "Jesus!" A cry of desperation, pure loneliness ringing out into the dark.

Between one blink of his eye and another, the darkness filled with stars. On every side, and above him and below him appeared myriad constellations and galaxies of shining white stars, skimming silently nearer, growing bigger and brighter.

He cried out wordlessly, fearing everything – the darkness, the stars, their speed, his aloneness – and then warmth, like invisible arms, wrapped him tightly round, wrapping him from the cold. The warmth sank into him, warming his blood, warming his bones, warming him into a drowsy peace. In an instant, the fear vanished and he floated, watching the thousand upon thousand of white stars come nearer and sprout beating wings. They were men and women with white wings. Angels, he thought, with no surprise. So there really are angels – and here they are. And they do have wings.

Flying, he thought. Underwater? Was he not in water then? Where was he? He didn't know, couldn't tell, and was too peaceful to care. He held out his arms to the coming angels.

Their arms reached out to him. Their wings beat and, in their hands, they carried spears. Helmets were on their heads, hair spilling out from beneath them. Round the waists of some were belted swords. On the shoulders of others were slung rifles. They came from everywhere, and they carried rocket-launchers, machine-guns, machetes, baseball bats. It was so strange to see angels wearing knuckle-dusters that he almost laughed –

170

and then wondered why. They had to fight the good fight, didn't they?

Closer still, and he looked into their faces, only to be dazzled by the light reflected from them – as if each approaching figure had a sun behind it, so that he saw only a blurred silhouette against a glare. On they rushed and he was buffeted by warm air, enveloped in a scent of honey and cinnamon. The air boomed with wing beats. The darkness turned to a glow and blur of white, and he was touched and brushed by a rustling softness. Hands reached for him, arms caught him, and he stopped with a jolt that made him realize he'd been falling all this time, falling and falling without knowing it. But now was saved.

Solid, strong arms went round him, and pressed him hard against the warm solidity of strong bodies. His face was pushed against warm, smooth skin, into feathers, against metal, into hair. They flew, with a constant boom and rustle of wings, and he was carried with them. Strange, he thought. Can this be real? There are no such things as angels, he thought, and flying with angels through a great darkness… It couldn't be real. But it was real. He could feel the angels, hear them, see them, smell their sweet, milky odour.

The angels wheeled, carrying him with them, all of them together sweeping round in a great circle. At the same time, they went down – and down, and down. Whirling round and down as if – and he wanted to laugh again – they were swirling down some unimaginably huge plug-hole. Looking down through the thrashing wings and legs, he caught a glimpse of a distant round glow of reddish light, as if he looked down into a long pipe, with light rising up into it. The round glow rushed upwards towards him, growing larger, glowing brazenly until at last, with a *whoosh!* of wings, his bearers burst from the bottom of the pipe and the glowing brazen circle became a whole wide brazen sky.

Below was mud. A land stretching away in every direction to meet the dull red sky, a land of grey mud. No other colour. Not a tree, not a bush, not a single leaf. No hills, no rivers, no walls. Nothing but flat, grey mud.

But as the angels dropped towards the mud – their great wings cupping and driving down the air with a *whump!* – something did come into view. A nest of snakes. Massive snakes. The great round bodies writhed, grey-brown in colour, out of the grey mud. The scales caught the reddish light of the sky and gleamed, dull copper, dull brass.

The angels wheeled, carrying Duncan, circling the knot of snakes, dropping nearer and closer. Snake mouths opened. Fangs flexed. Human eyes glared up. And there was Zoe, swaying among the snakes; and there was Mrs Beckerdyke – it was so ridiculous to think of her, here, in this place, as "Mrs Beckerdyke". But what else was he to call her? He called out – "Hey!" – and a tail rose from among the snakes and rattled with a whispering, scraping sound. He couldn't tell if the women were caught and trapped among the snakes – or if their legs had turned into snake's tails.

The angels let Duncan slip through their arms, and his feet sank into the grey mud. For a moment he felt he was falling, but then the sinking slowed, though he felt the mud clinging to and sucking at his legs. All around him the wings boomed and whirred as they held the angels above the mud.

And up through the mud came – oh God – such things. Fish-bodied things, fat and slimy, with crocodile mouths. Pale, transparent things, through whose faintly shining flesh could be seen hearts beating, veins pulsing and guts squirming. Torsos like men, with octopus tentacles for arms. Things with humped, spined backs, and things with mouths as wide as their heads and teeth as fine as fish-bones. Things which drew long fingered hands from the mud, and the claws on those hands drew out and drew out and drew out, and still weren't clear of mud. Things whose features vanished as they swelled and bloated before his eyes; things rotten and falling to pieces – scores of these things, hundreds of them, came up through the mud, with the mud clinging to them and sliding from them.

The stink was feculent, and overpowered the cinnamon and honey scent of the angels. Duncan fell back among the fluttering wings, covered his mouth and nose with his hand, turned his face into the white feathers about him, desperate to escape that stench. He knew for certain that all he saw was real, and no dream – who ever had a dream where they *smelt* things?

His face buried in a wing, he took a deep breath, and then shouted out, "Come away from there!" He shouted to the women. They couldn't wish to stay among those things, in that stink.

Neither answered him nor moved. They stared at him, over the heads of crouching things, and sagging things like frogs that weren't frogs, and things whose very shapes were changed by their slightest smirk or movement, bulging here, sinking in there.

Behind his hand, he caught at another breath. "Zoe! Zoe! Come to us!"

Zoe folded her arms and tilted up her head. She turned her back on him as a grey-brown, mud-covered snake coiled itself round her.

He despaired of her. Did she even see – or hear, or smell – where she was?

On either side of him, wings whirred, and angels hefted clubs and guns and swords. They looked to Duncan, as if waiting for his signal – but signal for what? A fight?

He didn't want to get any nearer to those filthy things than he was already. The thought of touching one, even to hit it, made him sick.

Elizabeth Beckerdyke, among the snakes, among the things, looked calmly at him, as if she stood among geraniums in a garden. She even smiled. "I'm astounded that you've reached here," she said. "You're a remarkably talented boy, did you know that?"

He shook his head, wondering at these strange words, the words of a teacher encouraging him to work harder. Was it a dream, after all, and was he putting into the dream words he'd like to hear?

"Come and learn," she said. "Are you afraid of a bit of dirt, a bit of ugliness? You'll never learn anything, Duncan, if you stay over there with the pretty things." She held out her hands to him. "Come and get some wisdom, dear."

"Mrs Beckerdyke," Duncan said, almost laughing at his own politeness, but feeling that he must be polite just the same, "I want Zoe back."

Elizabeth Beckerdyke smiled and, at her smile, every bloated, stinking, distorted, gaping thing rushed at him with teeth and stings, claws and stink. Duncan threw himself back, bringing up his arms to protect himself from raking talons and spittle and lashing, spiked tails. All around him, the air boomed and whirred as the angels rose; the air pushed by their wings shoved him and almost knocked him down; and through the din came the painfully loud crack and thump of guns firing, the splat of clubs striking into faces, the smack of swords and axes striking into flesh.

This is no dream, Duncan thought. No dream he had ever had, not even a nightmare, had been so all-surrounding, so full of vehement and variable noise and horrible detail. A gaping, blubbery face convulsed and spat yellow bile into the face of an angel, which melted. A froggish thing leaped and drove long, sickle-like claws through the meat of a white wing, slashing, and dragging the angel down in sprays of blood and feathers. Other wings thrashed above feet trapped in clenched jaws. A bitten arm was wrenched apart, bone from bone, at the elbow. Never for an instant did the noise stop – the booming of wings, the smack of weapons, the yells, the screams – nor did the roiling movement on all sides ever rest. From beneath a bloodied wing a dog-like thing that moved like an ape cantered at Duncan, its black, vaulted mouth agape, showing long yellow fangs and a scarlet tongue. He jumped aside from its bite, but it lashed out a hand and raked claws along the side of his thigh, right through the thick cloth of his jeans, tearing upwards from knee to hip.

The pain burned. The wounded leg weakened and sank beneath him, and the thing was standing over him, grinning with its dog-head, sitting back on its ape-haunches and reaching for him with its hands. A spear came out through its chest and pinned it into the mud. The angel driving down the spear hovered above, the beats of her wings rippling the mud's surface, as the dog-thing's hands clutched and scratched at the shaft protruding from its body.

I've got to fight! Duncan thought, and looked round for a weapon. A pinion slapped his face. A gust of stench choked him. Blinking through tears, he saw an axe sinking in the mud, and grabbed at it. The muddied shaft was thick, solid and slippery with mud, sliding through his grip. The axe-head was heavy and clumsy; hard to lift and hard to move. Why is it so heavy? he thought. If this is my dream, why haven't I dreamed it light and easy to use? Why don't I dream that I know how to use it?

A thing came flying at him through the air. Whether it was thrown, or something alive, he didn't have time to see. He tried to swing up the axe to bat it away, but his arms ached with the strain, and moved slowly, slowly... The thing, snapping, flapping, punched into his face, and over he went, backwards, slap into the mud.

Pain in his face as the thing bit, drove in its claws. He feared for his eyes. Then the thing's cold, wet weight was gone, and a strong, warm

arm pulled him to his feet. Momentarily he was enveloped in the peace of a white wing, and then battle broke in on him again. The noise, the confusion of movement, made him suddenly ferocious. I'll kill, he thought, forgetting pain. I'll mash all these filthy, vile slimy things. Chop them. Stomp them. I'll hack my way through to Zoe and slice them away from her.

He gripped the axe in both hands and swung it up – its weight had vanished; it was light as a stick. He was filled with a conviction of winning. The axe struck and burst a gelid body, splattering him with gobbets; he drove it into something more solid and twisted and wrenched it free. Above, beside, behind him, wings boomed and whirred, guns crackled, swords flashed down. A thing leaped at him and sank its teeth and claws through his arm, and clung weightily to him, its eyes glaring at him. An angel, wielding a long knife, severed the head of the thing from its body, but its head remained, fastened on his arm. With every movement, he had to struggle against its weight.

He was drenched with sweat, which was turning icy on his skin. Sweat and blood was running into his eyes, stinging and blurring his vision. He swiped with the axe at something he hardly saw, and felt it fall away. A gap opened in the mayhem and he glimpsed Zoe, standing quite still, her arms folded, her face sulky. She was his goal. He plunged for her, mad to reach her.

He rugby-charged past a bulk, shouldering it aside. Something sped past above his head, lifting his hair. Seeing his way blocked, he swung the axe in wide arcs, hardly taking in what stood in his way – a staring eye, a muscled side, a gleaming carapace with bristling hairs sprouting through it. Angels were with him. He heard their wings, glimpsed spears and swords, heard rifle-fire. We're winning, he thought, panting. It hurt to gasp in air.

There was Zoe, close enough to touch. A brown snake, glinting with dulled gold was coiled about her waist and looked at him over her shoulder – but she seemed unaware of the snake, or of the battle. With arms folded, she stared into the distance, as if impatiently waiting for someone. She hadn't noticed that she had no legs, only a snake's body – a body which led back to the writhing nest of snakes from which Mrs Beckerdyke rose, smiling at him and waving.

It was weird – everything was weird – but Duncan had no time to laugh. At the edge of the circle he and the angels had cleared, things were gathering again. He dragged in as much breath as he could and yelled, "Zoe!"

"She doesn't hear you," Mrs Beckerdyke said. "She doesn't wish to hear you. Why don't you give up and take a rest?"

The snake coiled around Zoe stared at him and shifted its head to watch him. Thinking that, perhaps, the snake had some power over her, Duncan hefted his axe and chopped through its neck.

"Oh!" Mrs Beckerdyke said. "*Big* mistake!"

The head fell into the mud and wallowed. He raised his eyes to see the severed neck healing over – and then sprouting two small buds which grew in seconds, as he watched, into two snake-heads.

An angel crashed into the mud, sending splashes of it everywhere. On the angel's chest was a dog-ape, tearing with teeth and claws. Another angel was being gulped down whole by a thing which was all mouth and belly, its belly clutching and remoulding itself about its prey, a wing sticking out of its mouth in a spray of white feathers.

Duncan swung the axe again, to chop off the snake's new heads. His arms were heavier. His legs dragged. He tried to draw his strength together and hack with as much energy as before, but the effort took still more strength from him. A weight landed on his back with a thump, and he felt knives, or something sharp, stab into his buttocks. The sharpness flexed, like clutching fingers. Something clawed had lodged itself on his back. Now it snarled in his ear, dampening his neck with its breath.

Twisting, he tried ridiculously to hit at the thing with the axe. His shoulder was painfully wrenched. The weight of the severed head still impaled on his arm dragged that hand from the axe – and then the weight of the axe dragged his other arm down, pulling at the muscles. The clawing weight on his back bore him down and he fell into the mud, shouting, "No, no, no!" – until the mud rushed into his mouth, silencing him.

Choking, he struggled to lift his face clear of the mud. He blinked, and mud clung to his eyelashes and bleared his sight, but he glimpsed humping, bounding shapes gathering round him. Terrified, he fought, trying to throw the weight off his back, trying to get his hands and knees under him and stand up, but the thing on his back clawed his shoulders and shoved him down, and he slipped in the mud and – worst of all – the dreadful weakness of exhaustion slackened his limbs.

His hair was gripped, and his whole scalp burned with pain as his head was dragged up. His arms were seized and he was thrown over on his back. He looked up into bulging red eyes that stared above a wide, wide mouth.

His arms were still held and were pulled on. The pain in his shoulders and across his back was intense. The pulling flattened his chest until he couldn't breathe, and still the pulling went on. He could feel the bones in his shoulders and elbows parting, little by little, and each little hurt more, but he couldn't cry out because he couldn't draw breath.

Knives flashed in the red light. The froggish things, the ape-dogs, the legged fish, were bringing swords and long knives. He saw one raised above him and screamed out against it, but the knife came down anyway. The pain went through him, dizzying his mind. For an instant he saw a vision of a table, a carpet and a gas-fire...

He fell into the mud. Thinking that at least one of his arms had been released, he tried to roll over – but when he tried to put his free arm beneath him, there was nothing. His arm had gone.

It was waved in his face by a grinning, dog-faced thing. *No!* he screamed, in his mind: *No, no, no!* He couldn't face that horror, didn't want to admit it...

They crowded round him, the things, dribbling on him, pushing him into the mud, sawing at him. He flashed in and out of pain: saw a television set, a mantelpiece, an old sofa...

They cut off his arms and legs, and were carrying them, like fishing-rods, over their shoulders. A dog-ape, stooping and holding him by the hair, set a long knife to his throat and sawed.

It carried his head to Beckerdyke and held it up to her.

Duncan looked out of his eyes still, though his

head dangled, bodiless. He watched Beckerdyke swing to and fro, but it was him who was swinging – a mere head – from the thing's paw.

Mrs Beckerdyke reached out and patted his cheek, which halted the swinging. He even felt the touch of her hand. "You're not strong enough," she said. "Yet."

The thing holding his head raised it higher. Duncan, rolling his eyes down, saw, below, a gaping mouth. He saw the teeth, and the ribbed top of the mouth, and the gullet opening. And then his hair was released and he fell straight into the open mouth – like a peanut tossed down at a party – and the mouth closed, and there was darkness.

Lightning flashes that hurt his head. Brilliant light, bursting in on him, like rolling waves, making him feel sick. He lifted his head, and everything swooped and wavered in front of him; and he felt sicker. Had he been drinking? God, had he fallen off the wagon and gone on a drunk again? It was like waking up after a bender – the slow-moving waves of nausea, the pain, the dry mouth and dizzy muzziness.

The pain was in his shoulder, not his head.

Squinting, he peered about him. He was kneeling on an old carpet, a grubby, grey old thing. A small room and, on the other side of it, an old sofa, and two doors. He was in Elizabeth Beckerdyke's little house where he had been – years ago. Years and years ago.

He clutched at his arms, looked down at his legs. He still had them. Lifting one arm, he was surprised that there was no head fastened to him by its teeth. Yet his arm was heavy and painful, as if the head was there.

There was Zoe, in the middle of the room, in the arms of the thing that she thought was Gary; and she was smiling, quite content to be there. Near them stood Elizabeth Beckerdyke, with that egg-smooth face. No snakes to be seen anywhere.

He felt as if he was dangling above a great dark drop, swinging and dangling, and there was nothing real or graspable anywhere about him.

Beckerdyke leaned towards him. To him she seemed to move slowly and ponderously, like a toppling tower. She whispered, "Better run away, little shit."

Leaning against the door behind him, he struggled to his feet, his legs almost too weak to raise him. Even when he was standing, he trembled and thought he would collapse, but gritted his teeth and stayed upright. Both Beckerdyke and the other thing, the Gary-thing, were staring at him, but made no move to come nearer. He turned, sliding against the smooth painted surface of the door, and managed to get it open even though he was leaning on it. Hugging his arm, he toppled through into the kitchen.

From behind him, Beckerdyke's voice shrilled, "Run away! He's run away! Christ's soldier – running away!" A door to the right of him led into the back yard. But how to open it? He didn't want to let go of his painful right arm.

As he watched, the door opened. He didn't feel surprised, only glad. And once through the door, it was only a step across the yard to the gate, standing open. He went down the alley as fast as he could, though he staggered dizzily, dreading falling against the wall and hurting his arm. He staggered into the street and across the pavement, fell against a parked car, just managing not to crush his wounded arm beneath him.

Looking around, he saw hedges, and full waste-paper bins, trampled old wrappers and discarded fast-food trays...

It was unreal.

11

GARY AND ZOE

Zoe and Gary were kissing. She had her arms tight around him, sliding her hands up and down his back, revelling in his warmth and his *thereness*. Gary's hand was hard at the back of her head. Their wet lips slid over and around each other.

Someone spoke behind her. "Zoe." She wasn't interested. She had Gary back, and pushed her tongue into his mouth. "Zoe!" The voice had sharpened.

And the body in her arms cooled. Her clutching arms dropped, empty. She opened her eyes and saw the wall in front of her, and the door to the stairs. No Gary.

She turned, seeing the drab little room. The rickety little table, the old sofa, the ugly little plastic chandelier. And Elizabeth Beckerdyke, standing in front of her with a mug in each hand. "I thought you might like a nice cup of tea," she said.

"Where's Gary?" Gary had been there. She looked round again, her mind rocking as everything of the past few minutes shifted and muddled. Gary *had* been there. She'd been holding him. She'd been so happy. It was like waking from dreams of a warm bed to find herself in the same bed, but a cold, single bed. "Where's he gone?" Her voice had risen sharply.

"Here." It was his voice, speaking from close behind her, into her right ear.

She turned quickly, but saw nothing except the shabbiness of the little room. It was as if, after speaking, he'd hurried away and hidden himself – but there was nowhere he could have hidden in so short a time. "Where are you?"

She heard him snigger – behind her again. She turned. He wasn't there.

"Sit down," Elizabeth Beckerdyke said, gesturing towards the sofa with one of the mugs.

"Where's Gary?"

"Don't get hysterical. Sit down."

Zoe sat, her legs sprawled. Arguing with Beckerdyke had never got her very far. She accepted a mug of tea.

Standing in front of her, and raising her own mug of tea before her face, Beckerdyke said, "Your Gary is never going to leave you again."

"Where is he?"

"Inside you."

Zoe said nothing, but scowled, suspecting some trick.

"Inside your head. In your heart, if you prefer to think of it in that sentimental way."

Zoe's face screwed up as tears started to come. She didn't want Gary inside her head, or in her heart. She wanted him in her arms. As the sobs rose in her, she felt the weight of arms encircling her, and smelt Gary – his smell of sweat and cigarettes. She turned her head, and his face was pressed into hers, his body was pressed against hers. He was beside her on the sofa.

"He's closer to you than ever," Beckerdyke said. "As close as your blood in your ear. Close as your nail to your fingertip. Close as one lip to the other; close as your tongue to your teeth. Hugging you all the time. Kissing you all the time."

Zoe happily leaned into Gary – and sprawled the length of the sofa. He wasn't there for her to lean on. Bewildered, she looked up at Beckerdyke.

"Whenever you need him," the witch said. "When you're lonely. Then he'll be there."

"I'm here," said the voice in her ear.

"Don't expect others to see him," said the witch.

"What's the good of that?"

Beckerdyke and Company watched her, and calculated their next words. "Nobody'll ever be able to take him from you." They saw her delight and relief. "He's watching over you all the time. Guarding you. Keeping you. He's your Guide."

Zoe pouted. She liked that, though she didn't want to admit it. "Guide?" It sounded special to have a Guide, made her feel looked after and comforted. But she would still rather have Gary.

"And in bed, at night, when it's dark – then you'll have Gary. Then you'll feel his arms and his warmth."

Zoe's face relaxed into a smile. She thought of Gary – all hers – close to her as her teeth to her lips – and no one else could see or hear him. No one else could take him away. "Really?"

"Truly," Beckerdyke said. "You've got talent. A strong talent."

Zoe looked up suspiciously. No one had ever told her she had a talent before.

"Only special people, of great talent, have Guides," Beckerdyke said. "You could help others."

Zoe's scowl came back. "Why should I? Who ever helped me?"

"It'd earn you money. Do it well, and you'd earn more than in some two-aisled supermarket. People pay to have their hands held while their palms are read. They pay to have their cards read.

189

They pay for pretty candles and bits of ribbon and nice smells and bits of pretty-coloured stone. For you that means nice clothes, a little car, a little place of your own."

"I can't read palms," Zoe said.

"We can teach you." Beckerdyke spoke, but there was an echo of the words inside Zoe's head. "A pretty girl like you," Beckerdyke said. "Exotic looking. With the right clothes, the right props, you'd pull the punters in."

"A little car?" Zoe said.

Beckerdyke smiled, but the smile didn't crease her face. "I promise you much more – much more – than a little car. If you tell the people what we want you to tell them."

"Tell them," said Gary's voice, inside her head, "what we want you to tell them."

12
THE HIGH STREET

Duncan passed the old red-brick school on the corner. Every step jarred his arm and shoulder and reverberated with pain in his head, and still, distractedly, he found himself looking for claw-marks on his legs, and a severed head with its teeth in his arm.

He edged between the steel roadside barriers on one side and, on the other, the crates of vegetables piled up outside the greengrocer's. The traffic lights at the crossing had stopped the vans and cars, and he crossed the black and white stripes on the road and – the pain from his arm screaming in his head – he walked round the corner of the big pub with its terracotta bears' heads, and bright pink and yellow posters advertising live bands.

And then he was walking up the High Street. Pain and dizziness and fear made every detail crystal sharp and bright. A tall Sikh in a deep-red turban, with a grey-streaked beard. A thin white woman, a cigarette in her mouth and white high-heeled shoes at the end of her jeans, pushed a pushchair with one hand and pulled along a toddler with the other.

Strings and skeins of people crossing the street. A baker's window displayed cream cakes and biscuits with smiling faces iced on them. A butcher's next door, with a blue-and-white striped awning and heaps of butchered muscle and fat in the window. An elderly black man waiting at a bus-stop. The entrance to a covered market, people thronging in and out. A young Asian man standing at his stall, which was hung with leather jackets. A party of teenage girls, some black, some white, running and giggling together.

A bus stopping, people pouring off it, people pushing to get on. Cars passing by, on both sides of the road, passing and passing, each with at least one person inside. Queues in shops, crowds on the pavements. A supermarket with fluorescent orange posters covering its windows, a chemist, a florist with women gathering round the buckets of bright flowers.

Between a charity shop selling old clothes and books for an animal hospital, and a shop selling clothes for babies, was a shop whose window held, at its centre, a white china hand with lines painted on it: the Life Line, the Love Line, the Money Line. Beside the hand was spread a deck of brightly coloured Tarot cards and, on its other side, rune stones. Behind these things were posters showing wizards, dragons and priestesses against stormy skies and sunsets. Cards with Celtic lettering announced the cost of having your palm read, or "a full Tarot reading". There were prices for "love candles" and "money candles".

Several teenagers, boys and girls, stood outside the window, fascinated, pointing at the things inside. Through the doors of the shop could be glimpsed other customers, bending over the display-cases of jewellery.

Duncan went on a few metres, until he reeled against the plate-glass of a shop selling greetings cards and teddy bears. Somewhere at the back of his mind was a notion of finding a hospital – but what would the nurses say about the head attached to his arm? More urgent was to find a place to sit down. Better still, lie down.

The church of Saint Mary Virgin was a couple of hundred metres up the street. A short distance, but only after an age of struggling through pain muffled with cottonwool and faintness did he reach it – and then he hadn't reached it, but only the pavement outside it. He had to go through the gates and up a gravelled drive, on legs that seemed operated by someone else. The church doors took all his weight and strength to push open. But inside there was peace. The thick walls reduced the noise of the busy, traffic-filled street outside to a remote burr. The light was dim and cool, the chill air scented with polish and flowers.

Duncan made it from the door to the nearest pew and there his legs buckled and let him down on to the wooden seat with a jar that pained his arm. The teeth must be biting deeper, he thought – but when he looked he saw, with surprise, that there was no head biting into his arm. With more surprise, he remembered having realized that earlier.

He slumped and, as his heartbeat slowed, beat by beat, the pain in his arm lessened, though it didn't go away. The whiteness of the church walls bore in on him. The tall walls were painted white, and the pews, the lectern, the choir stalls, were all of dark, polished wood. The windows were of blue, green, red, yellow glass, tinting the white walls with colour. Above the altar a large window showed a stained-glass picture of a very meek and mild Jesus, holding a lantern. He had a little goatee beard so you could tell he was a man – otherwise, with his long yellow hair and long robes, he might have been mistaken for the Saint Mary the church was named after. Could a Jesus like that fight the –? He looked down at his arm again, to remind himself that there was no head clamped there.

There was none to be seen now, but there had been a head. There had been things – vile things. He pressed his heels to the floor and felt the hard stone under his feet.

His hip-bones pressed against the hard wooden seat. No less real had been the stiff feathers of angels' wings against his face and hands, the bite of teeth and swords. Why was he here in a church with traffic passing outside, and not there, in the mud, fighting with the angels? There was no reason – for a moment he swung with his heart-beat, and everything around him swayed and shifted as if with a current of water.

He gritted his teeth and the fist of his uninjured arm, and the solidity of the church reasserted itself. But that was how close that other place was – a wavering of the sight, a dizziness, a moment's distraction… He knew that he would find himself in that place again.

Outside on the street were hundreds of people, going in and out of shops, getting on and off buses, driving in cars, happy in the idea that what they saw and touched around them was the one and only reality. He was unlucky enough – lucky enough? – to know it wasn't so.

The amiable, girly, smiling Jesus in the window above the altar could teach him nothing useful – and he needed to learn, quickly. Next time, he needed to be stronger, wiser, better prepared.

Mrs Beckerdyke could teach him. She'd offered to. Know your enemy.

He had to look at his arm again, to make sure that the jaws weren't clamped there, that eyes weren't glaring at him. Maybe he needed to learn what Mrs Beckerdyke knew, but he didn't want to learn it from her.

It was Jesus he needed, but not this pretty, oh-so-clean, untouched Jesus.

He needed a Jesus who'd been drunk and thrown up down his robe, who'd been in the cells on a drunk, who could fight as well as love.

The church, the window, the altar, all vanished in the haze of sun-dazzling brilliance, and a voice said in his ear, "Here I am."

Have you read?

THE STERKARM HANDSHAKE

From out of the surrounding hills came a ringing silence that was only deepened by the plodding of the pack-ponies' hooves on the turf and the flirting of their tails against their sides. Above the sky was a clear pale blue, but the breeze was strong.

There were four members of the Geological Survey Team: Malc, Tim, Dave and Caro. They'd left the 21st that morning at eight, coming through the Tube to the 16th, where the plan was to spend four days. None of them had ever been so far from home before, and they often looked back at the Tube. It was their only way back.

It was when they lost sight of the Tube among the folds of the hills, that trouble arrived.

Three horses, with riders, picked their way down the hillsides towards them. The horses were all black and thick-set and shaggy, with manes and tails hanging almost to the ground. The riders' helmets had been blackened with soot and grease, to keep them from rust, or covered with sheepskin so they looked like hats. Their other clothes were all buffs and browns, blending into the buffs, browns and greens all around them. Their long leather riding boots rose over the knee. On they came with a clumping of hooves and a jangling of harness, carrying eight-foot-long lances with ease.

"It's all right," Malc said. "Don't worry. They're just coming to check us out."

"There's others," Caro said. There were men on foot, about eight of them, running down behind the riders.

The riders reached them first, and circled them, making the geologists crowd closer together, while still clinging to the halters of the pack-ponies. The riders' lances remained in the upright, carrying position, but this wasn't reassuring.

Up came the men on foot, and the riders reined in to let them through. The footmen were all bearded and long-haired, and had long knives and clubs in their hands. A couple had pikes. Without any preamble, they laid hands on the ponies' halters and tugged them out of the geologists' hands.

"Don't argue," Malc said. "Dave, let it go. Let them have whatever they want."

Two of the riders dismounted, handing their reins to the third – a boy of about fourteen – who remained on his horse. They had a look of each other, the riders, like brothers. The first to dismount, his lance still in his hand, was probably the eldest. He was bearded, but no older than about twenty. He went straight up to Malc and began to pull the back-pack from his shoulders.

"I thought they'd agreed not to rob us any more," Caro said, taking off her own back-pack as the other dismounted rider came towards her.

"Just don't annoy them," Malc said.

As Dave and Tim shrugged out of their back-packs, one of the bearded footmen called out something – in a speech that sounded like coughing and snarling. His companions all laughed.

The geologists looked anxiously at each other. They didn't understand the joke, and were afraid of how far it might be taken.

The second dismounted rider suddenly caught Tim's hand and pulled his arm out straight. For a moment Tim looked into an almost beardless and strikingly pretty face – and then the young man was dragging at his wrist-watch, pulling the expandable bracelet off over his hand. He stared Tim in the face for a moment, and then snatched off the geologist's spectacles before moving on to

Dave and grabbing at his hands too. Dave took his wrist-watch off and gave it to him.

Malc and Caro, catching on, quickly took off their wrist-watches and handed them over.

The first rider – the bearded one handling an eight-foot lance as if it were a pencil – seemed not to like the pretty one having all the watches, and a coughing, snarling argument started between them. While it went on, Malc caught sight of Caro's face, set in a grimace of fright. The other two looked much the same, and he supposed that his own face also reflected his painful uncertainty and fear.

The argument ended with the pretty thief handing two of the wrist-watches to the one with the lance – who immediately turned to Malc, grabbed his waterproof and pulled at it, snarling something.

Malc pulled his waterproof off over his head. The others hurried to do the same.

The pretty rider gestured at their other clothes. Take them all off, he seemed to mean. Certainly, when they hesitated, there were more peremptory gestures and snarled words.

Caro saw the way the footmen gathered closer as she pulled off her jumper, and she stopped, only to be shoved, and staggered on her feet, by the horseman with the lance. When she still hesitated, he grabbed at her shirt, pulling the buttons undone and exposing her bra.

"Caro, do as they want," Tim said. "It'll be all right. We're here."

Malc, Tim and Dave all edged closer to her, trying to shield her, but she knew perfectly well that there was nothing they could do to protect her, outnumbered and unarmed as they were. She took off her shirt, shaking with fear. There was nothing remotely exhilarating about the feeling. She felt sick and desperate, and wished she'd never left the humdrum safety of the 21st-side.

They took off all their upper clothing, but still weren't undressing quickly enough for the liking of their attackers, who dragged at their arms, and pushed them, to hurry them up. One of the footmen, by pointing, made it clear that he wanted their boots – and then, when they were seen to be wearing thick socks, the socks were pulled off their feet, and their trousers tugged at.

They stripped down to their underpants, which caused hilarity, and the pointing and jeering was as threatening as the shoves.

Despite being so funny, their underpants were taken too, leaving the Survey Team standing naked in the breeze. Their skin roughened with goose-pimples.

Their attackers walked round them, examining them from all sides, pointing, making remarks and laughing. Caro closed her eyes and held her breath, feeling her heart thumping heavily under her breastbone.

But then the riders mounted again, and the whole party left with their loot, the footmen leading the pack-ponies.

The Survey Team were left, shaking but still alive, to walk over rough country, naked and bare-foot, all the way back to the Tube and the 21st.